I0742591

20!8

THE ORDER OF ATHENA

VS

the orange bastard

a novel by Anita Lobo

Buckman Publishing LLC
PO Box 14247
Portland OR 97293
buckmanpublishing.com

20!8: The Order of Athena Vs The Orange Bastard/ Anita Lobo and E.L. Hopkins

ISBN: 978-1-7323910-4-8
Library of Congress Control Number: 2019934231

This is a work of fiction. Names, characters, places, and incidents either are the products of the author's imagination or are used fictitiously. Any resemblance to actual persons, living or dead, businesses, companies, events, or locales is entirely coincidental.

Editor: E.L. Hopkins
Interior artwork: Hugh Newell
Cover and Interior Design: Eli Hopkins

Buckman Publishing
Portland, Oregon

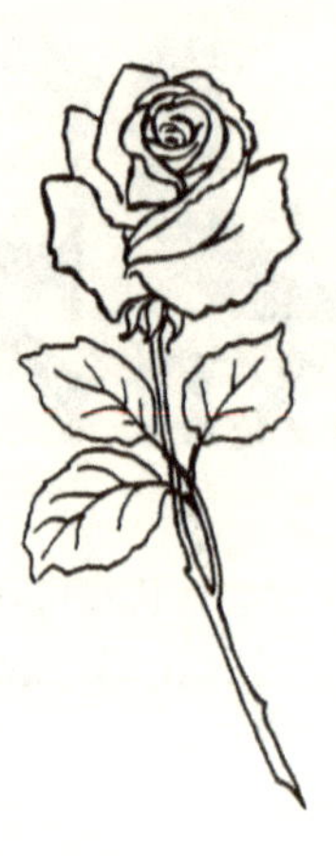

20!8

THE ORDER OF ATHENA

VS

the   orange   bastard

"It is she who saves the people as they go to war and come back. Hail, goddess, and give us good fortune and happiness!"

- some old, dead, white dude

Try to think about the weirdness. Try to remember the little things that didn't make sense. The person walking behind you who suddenly isn't there anymore, the missing keys you know you left on the table. The things that just barely exist on the periphery of your mind. All the little things that you know are off, but your brain decides to forget. If you didn't forget you'd have to face the possibility that things are not what they seem, or that you're insane. A lot better to just forget and move on. Well at a certain point it hurts less to let go than it does to hold on.

And when that happens, The Sisterhood is here for you.

Look for us. Find us. Join us.

The Order of Athena

It was never supposed to be like this. *Yeah, no shit*, you're probably thinking. But, like, really, it wasn't. I'm going to tell you something unbelievable, but once you've heard it, it will make so much sense that your head will spin. Or rather it will stop spinning. Hopefully. Stringing words together isn't really my forte, so you'll have to bear with me. Personally, I'd be much happier karate chopping the necks of my enemies, be they orange or otherwise. But instead I'm trying to put this all together for you.

You probably think you know all about Cleopatra, Joan of Arc, Dorothy Parker, Maya Angelou, Hillary Rodham, etc...well if you actually knew the truth your head would explode (I know, I'm only a hundred words in and I've already perpetrated two separate but equally clichéd head-related metaphors; I throw myself at your mercy). So put on your helmets, because I'm going to tell you the true history of the world. Now, I'm no neurologist, but I think a helmet should probably do the trick.

Who am I? Don't worry about that for now.

You might be wondering, why spill the beans now? After centuries of absolute (well, mostly absolute) secrecy? Well, shit is going down. Big time. That's why. Unforeseen shit that will almost definitely change the course of human life as we know it. And because gossip is my second favorite thing after karate chopping the necks of my enemies. If the worst happens (which, if you've been paying attention, "the worst" turned out to be nothing more than an appetizer; a profiterole before a coq au vin, and goddamnit now I'm hungry again) you need to know how it happened so that you can stop it from happening again. Or at least fail with excellent style.

And to be completely honest, I could really use the cash from the book sales.

The Order of Athena is a sisterhood that stretches beyond the limits of known history, and has been at the bleeding edge of virtually every major historical event you can think of (except stuff like the Holocaust and Vietnam, which is what happens if we're not there to control the boy's club). Membership in The Order is both an honor and a burden, but that's how it goes when you run the world. Certain male types have been periodically allowed on the inside, so to speak, provided they're able to understand the subordinate nature of their roles. And if for some reason they forget themselves and get too big for their trousers? Well, let's just say that accidents happen, all the time... achoo! *Lincoln*. Damn this drafty office.

Well, I could just go on and list the achievements and highlights of The Order, but that would be boring, and I currently have a lot of time on my hands so I'd rather just show you what's happening.

Codename: Sarah P.

∞September∞

I poured a generous splash of merlot into the cleanest looking juice jar I could find, and shuddered when I heard Todd pull up outside on his snowmobile, which is his primary means of transportation, even in the complete absence of snow. I'd hoped to reach a nice stupor before he got home, as that tends to make our interactions a little less excruciating. Maybe have enough time to fire up my surveillance satellite, find a nude beach somewhere, rub one out.

I hate merlot. Can barely swallow it. But I'd gotten about ten gallons as a gift from my in-laws, who know nothing about my true identity. Or about wine, apparently. Virtually no one knows my true identity, including Todd, my hapless and by all accounts illiterate husband. I'd actually spilled the truth a couple times, both alcohol-fueled moments of misguided honesty. Probably there'd been a key-bump or two involved. Either he'd forgotten, or hadn't been listening in the first place. Either possibility was equally plausible.

Being required to actually procreate with Todd had been the greatest sacrifice so far, and the least savory. Diluting my genetic line with his was enervating beyond all reason. I've still never been satisfactorily convinced of the necessity (why him?) and over time I've become convinced it was part of some elaborate practical joke (or revenge?).

Bristol is the only one who actually knows the truth, but due to her father's genetic influence she lacks the intelligence to understand. Fortunately, her silence was cheaply purchased with outlet mall shopping trips to Coach, Banana Republic, and other second-rate purveyors of discount designer goods.

"What's for dinner?" Todd asked, coming inside and stomping mud on the hardwood floors I'd just finished polishing. He smelled like a combination of pine sap and diesel fuel, maybe a hint of moonshine.

"You're going to have to fend for yourself." I told him. "I have a flight in an hour."

"Not easy being married to a Governor." Todd chuckled. "Governess?"

"Governor." I said.

I hadn't actually been Governor for several years. A fact which Todd has characteristically failed to notice. I'd been ordered to resign when the duties of running even a backwater like Alaska had proven prohibitive to my real duties (not to mention the serious dearth of time left for my skin-care regimen).

"We got any more of them pork-n-beans?" Todd asked, cracking a beer.

"You know we do."

"Hot damn!"

Sometimes I'm envious of how easily he's able to achieve happiness, when it's always been so elusive for me. But my work is more important than happiness, I know.

After packing a couple bags (I only expected to be away for one night, but a girl needs options) I threw in a special polymer pistol that is invisible to security screening. Not even HR knew about the weapon, which was ostensibly worthless to me since my targets typically need to appear as if they've died of natural causes. But having it makes me feel safe. Not even a highly trained agent such as myself is immune to the gun mania so ubiquitous in my little corner of the U.S.'s second least contiguous state.

"You need a ride to the airport?" Todd asked, looming in the doorway, sniffing at something he'd dislodged from inside his ear.

"No, thank you." I grimaced. "I'm not sure when I'll get home, could be late tomorrow."

"That's fine. I probably shouldn't be driving anyway." He said, cracking his third beer in the few minutes since he'd gotten back from wherever he'd been. I'm pretty sure he's having an affair, and for this I'm grateful because it means avoiding the less savory aspects of our marital sham.

"See you when you get home?" He called out, grabbing two more beers and heading for the shower. The fact that he was showering was further proof of his infidelity, as personal hygiene has never been a priority for him (I present as evidence our wedding photo, in which his shirt is clearly speckled with deer blood).

A truck pulled into the driveway as I was loading my bags in the trunk.

"Hello, Levi." I sighed, avoiding eye contact.

"Ma'am." He said, tipping an invisible hat. "You need a ride anywhere?"

"No, thank you. I'll probably just take the car I'm currently packing."

"That's fine." He said, with obvious relief. "I probably shouldn't be driving anyway."

"So, don't."

"Is that an invitation to stay the night?"

"I suppose it is." I sighed. "She can't get pregnant again, right?"

"That's true," he agreed. "At least not until next year anyway."

"Won't that be nice."

A Steamy Encounter

Sitting at a wrought iron table outside a café in Monterey, California I zipped up my jacket against the late summer chill and gazed into the vast gray undulating expanse of ocean. Or at least what I could see of it through the trees and the throngs of disaffected tourists drifting aimlessly between boutiques selling various artisanal nonsense. Visually scrutinizing the crowds, always keeping an eye out for counteragents. I saw a cruise ship moored off the coast, the passengers barely visible through the oceanic fog.

The view reminded me of the seven stupidest words I've ever spoken: "I can see Russia from my house". I'd damn near blown my cover with that one. *Would have* blown my cover, if anyone had actually thought about what I'd said (maybe I was unconsciously trying to blow my cover; not that I'd stopped believing in my mission, I was just tired of being made fun of all the time, and I was also concerned about the toll being taken on my family; especially my daughter, who'd become a bit too comfortable with our less than gentile lifestyle). However, thinking critically about what people say had been out of fashion that season, and my cover remained intact. The truth is I *can* see Russia from my house, thanks to a stealth satellite, with which I'd been keeping a close eye on the Kremlin, as well as a variety of nude beaches with less than stellar security.

I saw my contact approaching from the south and applied a fresh layer of lipstick. Then I remembered that I'd already just done so, my lips now caked and gummy. I would've wiped some off on my knockoff Shahtoosh scarf but Valerie P. was already approaching the table.

"What's up with your lips?" She asked, first thing.

"Shut up, Valerie."

"What're you gonna do?" She smirked. "Blow my cover? Again? Seems like all you're really good at."

"I'm also good at karate chopping your neck."

"How could I forget?"

"How was the boat ride?"

"Moist."

"Please don't say that word around me."

"Almost as moist as your panties when you're spying on nude beaches."

"Don't say that word either."

"What, *beach*?"

"Panties."

"You're so uptight," she rolled her eyes. "I can barely even exist around you."

"Perfect."

"You seem especially edgy today. You quit smoking or

something?"

"When I agreed to go undercover I didn't realize it was going to be for life." I confessed. "It's wearing on me. And Bristol is pregnant again. And yes, I quit smoking."

"She takes her cover pretty seriously."

"I'm afraid she's gone totally native. But that's not why I called this meeting."

"I'm the one who called the meeting."

"Whatever. Let's have a drink, it's been a long day."

"It's barely nine a.m."

"Like I said."

When the waiter came out with a pair of bloody mary's I glanced involuntarily at the prominent bulge in his slacks and didn't immediately notice the bar-towel he was gripping in one hand. The towel had presumably been white at one point, but was now as red as the drinks. He was wincing quite a bit.

"How much blood did you say you wanted in these?" He asked hopefully.

"None."

"I was afraid you'd say that." He grimaced and took the drinks back inside.

"Juicy young man." Valerie said. "Looks a bit like Levi."

I realized she was right and shuddered. Wondered if HR knew about that one unfortunate night.

"Don't worry," Valerie said. "Your cover is too important to be derailed by one indiscretion. But talk about an indiscretion. When you go off the rails, you really go off the rails, if you catch my drift." She smiled, tapping her nose.

"Did you bring me all the way out here just to judge me?"

"No, just a perk. If you get my meaning."

"A perk? Rails? Jesus Christ, Valerie. Do you want some blow? Is that what you're getting at?"

"Of course not. Unless you have some…"

Half an hour later we were sitting on towels in a steam bath off Cannery Row. Which in retrospect wasn't really the most ideal setting for a coke party.

"So," I said, sniffing and wiping sweat out of my eyes. "What's the deal?"

"Things are happening fast." She said, handing me a familiar looking envelope. "It's time to reactivate you."

"I thought I was active."

"Hardly. HR wants you in Arizona yesterday. There's a high profile target who needs to be eliminated."

"Not Maverick?"

"I'm afraid so."

"Isn't he dying anyway?"

"Not fast enough. He's losing control, and he's starting to talk."

"Shit." I said, unsealing the steam-limp envelope and reading the terse contents of the stationery inside.

"Don't worry," Valerie told me. "He knows all about it, and he's on board. He specifically said that he wants it to be you."

"That doesn't really make it any easier."

"What went on between you two, anyway?"

"Nothing. Don't worry about it."

"If you say so. Anyway, let's get out of here. My hair is getting destroyed."

"Oh, Valerie," I said as casually as possible under the circumstances. "There's one more thing written on this note."

Valerie looked at me. I saw a wave of realization crash over her face as she went for the tonto knife she had hidden under her towel. But she wasn't fast enough to avoid the edge of my hand as it karate chopped her in the neck and she collapsed on the tiled floor. I poured a ladle of botanically infused water over the heated rocks and her lifeless body disappeared in a cloud of lavender-scented steam.

So long, Valerie.

Festiva Nights

While waiting for my rental car I considered calling home and letting my family know I wouldn't be back as soon as expected, but decided against it. They're not the kind of people you want to feed too much information. It just confuses them. Besides, they're also not the kind of people who are likely to notice a discrepancy of a few days, so long as there's plenty of beer and pork-n-beans around. Which there is.

I hoped a long drive might be just the thing to get my head straight. Of all the targets I've taken down, none of them have ever been someone I'd consider a friend, until now. I didn't like the idea. Of course, I rarely like ideas that aren't mine, so that's nothing new.

There was also a question of wardrobe. Aside from a pair of flats I'd already lost while walking on the beach, the only shoes I had were the strapless Manolos I was currently wearing. And stunning as they were, they lacked the kind of tactical efficiency I'd require if I got into anything hairy. I made a mental note to swing through any discount malls I saw on the way. This was risky in itself, as the only times I ever seem to get recognized are at discount malls.

Since I hadn't arranged a car ahead of time, all they had

left was an ancient looking Ford Festiva. But I didn't want to cause a scene and risk being recognized, so I took the car and headed southeast into the desert.

Listen, Sisters: Would I have taken this gig if I knew what intricate and sometimes devilishly specific humiliations it would entail? If I knew that I, in perpetuity, would be the laughing stock of American politics (the only good thing about the current administration was that I no longer seemed quite as bad in comparison)? That I would be an unknown and unappreciated martyr whose public face would be a perpetual target of metaphorical—and sometimes literal— pies? That I would be saddled with a family whose illiteracy and basic lack of common decency would trouble my sleep nightly? That I would wake up drenched in sweat, never knowing what the next humiliation would be?

I mean, yeah, I would. Because despite what you think you know about me, old Sarah P. is a team player, who cares about making the world a better place for women, and who's willing to suffer the slings and arrows of outrageous fortune if it means little girls of the future can grow up without having their very existence under constant threat. And because if you've ever looked Ruth Bader Ginsberg in the eyes, her forehead drawn up by the extraordinary tightness of her bun, her neck-doily flapping majestically in the autumn breeze, you just don't say no to her.

You just don't.

There's also the fact that I get to kick the asses of a lot of dudes whose asses seriously need to be kicked. And yeah, there might've been some slight kind of warning about what might or might not happen to me if I betrayed the trust I'd already been shown, but that's neither here nor there.

And I guess the fact that I'm publishing this book means that my martyrdom is at least no longer unknown. Of course, I've noticed that people who claim martyrdom are sometimes treated with less deference than they'd hoped, and perhaps even mocked outright. But you know I'm already used to all that. It rolls off me like Donald Trump rolls off a freshly molested game bird.

I parked the car about a mile away from the house. The only thing worse than being caught assassinating a war hero and one time presidential hopeful would be the same situation, except this time everyone knows I was driving a Ford Festiva. The sun was setting over the scarred wasteland of desert in the west, the sky a brilliant rose colored band stretched tight across the horizon. I sat in the car waiting for darkness, listening to my favorite mixtape.

I stopped the tape just before Stevie Nicks' *Landslide* started, which was better listened to after the deed and not before. Listening to *Landslide* before killing someone can really throw you off, as I've learned the hard way.

Making my unsteady way across the desert in heels, I wished I'd gone with the Louboutins. Not that they're any more comfortable or sensible, but they're better for hiding bloodstains. Not that there was going to be any blood—there was specifically and explicitly not going to be any blood—but I like to be prepared. Except that I'm not, in this case, so never mind.

Approaching the walled in estate, I kneeled down and took inventory of my gear bag. Probably should've done that in the car where there was plenty of light, but this job had me a bit rattled. In addition to a syringe loaded with a serum that would replicate a heart attack, there was a bag of jerky that was infused with a powerful sedative. That was for the dogs. If Mav's beloved dogs got hurt he would definitely haunt me from the afterlife.

I waited for the guard to pass by and blew on my dog whistle. When the dogs came near I lobbed a couple pieces of jerky through the bars in the fence. But then the guard suddenly reversed direction and made another pass and I had to duck behind a shrub.

Thank god for that oddly placed, me-shaped shrub, I thought.

Before either of the dogs could get ahold of the jerky, the guard found and promptly ate both pieces. I hadn't expected that. It might've been a lucky break, except for the fact that I was counting on the guard to unlock the door to the house, which he did every other lap around the estate, using a thumb-print activated security door. Kind of hard for him to do that while lying face down in the remarkably well-manicured grass, where I knew he would stay for the next few hours at least. I wasn't sure how I was going to get inside now, but I still needed to incapacitate the dogs so I lobbed in another piece of jerky.

The guard, rousing himself with superhuman effort, had just enough energy to grab the other piece of jerky and eat that too.

Sweet Jesus. Unless I chopped off his thumb there was no way to open the security door, and there were still a couple dogs to deal with. Not to mention I was quickly running low on jerky. Shit, only one piece left, I realized, chewing thoughtfully.

Wait, *chewing?* Sonofabitch. I spit out what bits of the jerky I hadn't already swallowed, climbed shakily to my knees, and started scaling the fence. My only hope was that the dogs would remember me, despite the fact that I hadn't been to the house in over a year. Specifically, that they would remember me, but not remember how I'd kicked one of them for knocking a glass on red wine on my white silk skirt that one Easter.

When I landed on my back in the soft grass the wind got knocked out of me, along with a partially masticated chunk of jerky, which was the only good news I'd had in a while. I must've fallen asleep for a minute because suddenly there were hot dog tongues all over my face, and other places I'd rather not mention. So they remembered me, at least. Now all I had to worry about was figuring out how to climb a two-story veranda in a pair of strapless Manolos while drugged up on dog jerky.

Easier than it looked, actually! Though I hadn't counted on the window being locked.

Jimmying the window open with a hairpin, I felt a bit dizzy and plunged forward onto something that felt like a bunch of sausages wrapped in an old newspaper. Leaning up on one elbow I found my penlight and shined it on John McCain's face. His eyes were wide open and he wasn't breathing.

Time is an insidious and undefeatable enemy, kept at bay only with clean living and (since clean living wasn't in the cards for me) a top notch skin care routine. One good thing about the long dark winters up north: limited skin exposure.

I rolled off of him, not for the first time, and lay there in the dark, listening. His wife was visiting her sister in Tennessee so the house should've been empty, aside from Maverick and the guard. The guard was still unconscious in the yard, so I knew that if I heard anything it could only be an enemy. I waited for a few minutes but didn't hear anything other than the sound of my own blood pounding in my ears, and a Beyoncé hook that was stuck in my head.

When I finally turned on the light I looked at my old friend and running-mate lying there, his body already cold. My mouth tasted sour, like a combination of vomit and jerky, with just a hint of geriatric Republican.

Not good!

I was trying to figure out what to do when I heard the whine of sirens in the distance. And not the cool, oceanic sirens that tricked horny sailors into crashing their stupid ships. These were police sirens. The kind of sirens that meant bad news for old Sarah P. if she got caught hanging out with the corpse of a U.S. senator. I figured the best thing to do would be to go back out the window. Which meant climbing over Maverick one last time. It wasn't my favorite thing to do.

I had one leg hanging out the window when I saw a sheet of stationery that had fallen under the bed. It was a very specific type of stationery. The type that you're supposed to destroy once you've read it. It was the kind of stationery that you only see when HR wants you to take care of some business. I grabbed the paper and sort of rolled myself out the window, grabbing the lattice, which turned out not to be as sturdy as it looked. My heel got caught and broke off and the lattice and I had what would probably have been an hilarious fall, had it been happening to someone else.

It was a long walk back to the Ford Festiva, let me tell you.

Flight of the Intruder

I woke up from a nightmare, not knowing where I was. In and of itself this was nothing new for me, and normally I wouldn't have been bothered. Except this time something was different. Looking around the first class cabin I tried to figure out what it was, and then I realized. The seats were a different color. When I'd boarded, the seats had been an appalling cross between navy and periwinkle. I knew this for a fact because I'd been troubled by how they clashed with the blue in my arm veins. Now they were a deep dark gray, which was more flattering to my skin tone, so on the one level I wasn't complaining. But still. I pushed the button to summon a flight attendant.

"This might sound strange," I said, realizing only then exactly how strange it was going to sound. I almost aborted but I was already committed to saying something, and I couldn't think of anything else. "Weren't these seats a different color a minute ago?"

He looked at me the way you might look at a cat that had thrown up on your pillow.

"Are you suggesting we swapped out all the seats midflight?" He asked. "Or perhaps merely reupholstered them?"

"No." I said. "Of course not. But on the other hand, did you?"

He didn't immediately respond, and I decided to drop the whole thing in case he thought my line of questioning warranted cutting off my drinks. Despite being in first class, where asking seemingly bizarre questions should've been one of the privileges, I had my priorities.

"Nevermind," I told him. "Just bring me a vodka-soda."

"Hey, aren't you Tina Fey?"

"No." I said, an icy edge creeping into my voice. I'd met Tina a few times, unofficially. She was an amazing woman, and we got along much better than our appearance on Saturday Night Live would suggest. That said, it was hard not to take her satirical version of me personally.

"That's too bad." He said. "I love her. Her impression of Sarah Palin is spot on."

"If you say so."

"Talk about an idiotic piece of shit. I can't believe McCain let her get so close to the White House."

"Vodka-soda please!"

"I'm sorry, we're about to begin our landing sequence. No more drinks."

"What'd you do with the seats you sick fuck!"

Life is full of these moments. Unexplainable events that you either choose to ignore and forget, or else lose your mind dwelling on them. Whether it's that the world is constantly playing jokes on us, or our minds are rotting away, it really doesn't matter that much. Not as much as who wins on The Bachelorette, for example. Or whether your furniture clashes with your arm veins.

When I got home, Bristol was reading to Levi and Trig in the kitchen and I smelled something cooking that wasn't pork-n-beans, all of which filled me with suspicion. Also, shouldn't there have been a few more kids around?

"Oh, thank God!" Bristol shouted, tears in her eyes, as she came to embrace me.

None of this was normal.

"What're you doing?" I asked. Nobody seemed to notice that I'd been gone several days longer than expected.

"They said on the news that your plane almost crashed! Weren't you scared?"

"What? I don't know anything about that. What's going on here, anyway?"

"Reading." Bristol said. "I found this box of Berenstain Bears books in the attic. They're pretty cool."

"Berenstein," I corrected her. "Beren*stein* Bears."

"No," she said. "It's Berenstain. Look." She showed me the cover of the book. Sure enough: Berenstain. I felt dizzy and tried to brace myself on the half-built motorcycle Todd keeps in the kitchen. Except it wasn't there and I fell and knocked over the dog's water bowl, which actually had water in it. What the hell was going on here?

"Where's your father?" I asked, climbing to my feet.

"He's volunteering at the church."

"What the shit are you talking about? Todd's never worked a day in his life, and certainly not for free."

"Are you feeling okay, Mom?"

"Fuck this," I said. "I'm going snowmobiling."

"There isn't any snow, Mom. Summer's barely over."

"Fuck!"

Nothing made any sense. My husband was volunteering, my daughter was showing concern for my well-being? And when did she learn to read, anyway?

And fucking *Berenstain*? That was the last straw. Those were my favorite books when I was in college, and I knew for a fact that it was Beren*stein* Bears. I felt sick to my stomach. I needed a key-bump to get my head straight. Rifling my jewelry box, I experienced a brief but visceral moment of panic. But there it was. At least some things never change.

"Oh, Mom," Bristol's voice suddenly assailed me.

"What is it?" I snapped a bit too brusquely, wiping my nose.

"Sorry to startle you, but this came in the mail for you." She handed me a book shaped object wrapped in plain brown paper.

"What is it?" And when did she start using fancy words like *startle*.

"Well, I don't know, it's wrapped in brown paper."

"Right."

"Are you sure you're feeling okay?"

"No."

That was twice now that she'd asked me, which was twice more than anyone had ever asked before. Something was definitely up.

I continued unpacking, trying to put off the moment at which my mind would crumble under the weight of too much weirdness. Then I found the sheet of stationery I'd snagged while falling out of McCain's window. As far as I could tell, it was identical to all the other communiques I'd received from HR, except that its tone was a bit more genial and personal than those I typically received:

Mav, thank you for the heads up regarding possible counteragent, henceforth known as The Hacker. Have to admit, difficult to believe what you've told me, but you've never delivered anything less than perfect intel in past and have no reason to think otherwise now. Also, and I should've said this first, but overjoyed that you're in recovery. Would've been very sorry to lose you as an operative, and as a friend. Very glad I won't have to. --HR

Weird News Is Bad News

The next day was unseasonably warm and it rained all morning, melting what little snow had fallen overnight. I spent the morning unpacking and flipping through the channels waiting to hear something on the news about Mav's death. I suspected that the official story would eschew the more embarrassing stuff, like his being naked and whatnot. But not only did I see no heavily redacted version of the story, I didn't see anything about it at all. Though there were a few mentions of my plane, which had apparently almost crashed. Several less charitable anchors mentioned what a shame it was that it hadn't crashed, considering I was on it. I made a mental note of their names.

Then I remembered that the internet existed, and I looked him up. Every source I could find was saying that he had died peacefully in his sleep, almost three months ago. I couldn't believe what I was seeing. Of course, I knew that most of what gets reported is untrue in one way or another, but this was something else. How could they get away with pretending he hadn't been seen by countless elected officials at various house sessions and other less official Beltway get-togethers?

Between this and the Berenstain thing it was starting

to seem pretty obvious what was going on. I mean, when I really looked at the evidence there was only one possible answer: there had been a rift in the time/space continuum.

I needed fresh air, and felt in the mood for a drive.

While running some errands, wondering what to make of the whole Berenstain/Berenstein conundrum, I ran into a former classmate at the Foodmart. Goth Noir, he used to call himself. And apparently still did, according to his nametag. This level of weirdness in people over a certain age just reeks of death. And not in a cool goth way. In a gross, old way. His real name was Garth, named after pop-country legend, Garth Brooks. I always suspected that he'd had a crush on me, though I can't imagine why. I was about as goth as a scorpion bolo-tie. Which now that I think about it, it kind of makes sense.

He was pretty zoned out, most likely stoned, methodically stacking cans of meat product. One of those weird things I mentioned is that so many of the reasonably intelligent and diligent classmates I had grown up with should now be working in a second rate grocery store, while I should be, well, what I am. I try not to think too much about it. I might lose what's left of my mind if I did. I was taught early on that caring about other people is weakness, and weakness is how you end up spending your life stocking shelves with the sort of canned goods that only my husband will eat (despite spending most of his waking hours in morbid pursuit of woodland creatures, he never seems to put any of them on the table). For someone as petty as myself, to see my once illustrious and promising former classmates reduced to stocking shelves should be a source of comfort. But for some reason it wasn't working. Maybe because their failure juxtaposed against my success means that I don't really know very much about how the world works. Or maybe I have more empathy than I'm given credit for. My only explanation is that anyone smarter than me would've given up a long time ago, yet here I am. Though to be honest, "too stupid to give up" is not the epitaph I would prefer to see emblazoned on my presumably ostentatious headstone.

"Hey Garth." I said when he saw me. He cringed at the sound of his birth name. "I mean, Goth. Are you, uh, still playing music?"

He proceeded to tell me far more about electronic dance music than I ever needed or wanted to know, and I didn't retain a word of it.

"Sounds great." I said, shoving an armload of the cans he'd just finished stacking into my cart. "See you around."

I'd hoped to extricate myself without any further awkward encounters, but then I ran into my former best-friend, Kelly Whitney. She pretended not to see me, which was ridiculous considering she was working at the cash register where I was checking out. She's hated me ever since I nailed her boyfriend, and brother (separate people, I feel the need to mention) in high school. Petty bitch, right? And maybe her dad. Which might've had something to do with her family splitting up and her not going to Cornell at the last minute.

She still had basically the same face as back then—incredulous, accusatory—but, you know, old looking. And kind of washed out. Like she'd never recovered from having her dream life inadvertently derailed at such a critical age. But she didn't need to have such an attitude about it, is what I'm getting at. Especially not when I'm potentially dealing with some kind of interdimensional paradox. Frankly a little support would've been nice. But I guess she didn't know about any of that stuff (or much of anything else for that matter; I still don't understand how she got into Cornell; I mean, yeah, she was our class valedictorian, but she still couldn't stop her best friend from seducing her father, so how smart could she be?) so I tried not to judge her too harshly.

Her eyebrows though, that's a different matter. I was judging those permanently surprised looking arches as harshly as I've ever judged anything, which is saying a lot. I'm thinking about writing a letter to the newspaper.

"Hello, Kelly." I said, wishing I'd chosen a different

moment to restock on Todd's pork-n-beans, which he'd decimated in the few short days I'd been gone. Though judging from the miasma emanating from Bristol's room, I was guessing that Levi had provided some assistance.

"Hi, Sarah." She said, curtly eyeing the many brightly labeled cans, as I knew she would. Even when I was Governor I let her get away with calling me by my first name, because that's just the kind of person I am. But I'm also the kind of person who keeps a record of each instance, in case I feel less magnanimous in the future. "You might want to be careful eating too much of this stuff, it can really wreak havoc on your digestion."

"Yeah, I know. Believe me." For some reason I couldn't think of any witty comebacks, which everyone knows is my forte. I guess I was too preoccupied with the whole rift in the time/space continuum thing. Or maybe I felt something like sympathy for her, with her garbage life and her eyebrows, though that doesn't really sound like me. Probably it was just the time/space thing.

"So, what're you gonna do now that you quit being governor?" She asked, her words issuing from somewhere in the area below her eyebrows, which I couldn't look away from. "I guess the normal thing would be to get some kind of talk show."

"Well, I have been called the Dominic Dunne of

southern Alaska."

"Really? By whom?"

"Never mind that. The point is that we're both living up to our potential. And I want you to know how much I admire the way you've dealt with the whole Cornell thing. It can't be easy."

"Are you feeling okay?"

"Why does everyone keep asking me that?"

"Well, I can't answer for everyone else. But you know I never got into Cornell. I never even applied. My dad got cancer junior year and I decided to stay here and take care of him after my mom took off with my gymnastics coach. Actually, and maybe this is a weird time to bring this up, but I never thanked you for your help. I guess I was embarrassed, which is why I've been avoiding you all this time. And, well, I just hope that you can forgive me."

"Yeah, sure." I said. "Of course. Don't mention it. Listen, I just remembered I left the oven on, please excuse me."

I was lying about the oven, I think, but the truth was I had in fact been forgetting things. I'm pretty sure. When you're a forgetful person it's hard to remember whether or not you've been forgetting things, and what those things might've been. For example, I forgot that there used to be another kid around the house (or two?) in addition to Bristol and Trig (not counting Levi, as I have personal reasons for choosing not to think of him as a kid). And even more noteworthy, I'd forgotten about the parcel I'd received. This was highly unusual, as I tend to immediately rip open packages like an impatient kid on Christmas morning, even when the name on the package is a name other than mine. In this case there hadn't actually been any name on the package, but there had been an address, which was my address.

When I got home I immediately unwrapped the parcel I'd received. In a million years I would never have guessed what it contained.

Harsh Dairy

The package, as I've previously noted, was very discretely wrapped in brown paper, which turned out to be a to-go bag from Burger King. At first I thought Todd was ordering soiled underwear from Korean girls again (I told him to at least stop using my DHL #). But It turned out to be a diary. Of sorts. I've done my best to transcribe what I feel to be the most relevant parts, and in the absence of relevance, the funniest. Much of it was written in crayon, and not a particularly well sharpened crayon. At first I thought it was the kids, but they don't write anything down anymore. It's all computer video sex games with kids these days. And I know for a fact that my kids don't even know how to write. That might be partially my fault, considering they were all homeschooled.

What follows is the first page I read:

Dear Dairy,

Sad again today. Couldn't do anything with my hair and stubbed my toe on dresser, and really hurt! Then ate half a cheesecake and threw up in the elevator. Think I'll stay in bed all day. Told SS (Secret Service) don't feel good, which I guess true? Haha! Just remembered Gossep Gurl back on Netflix, if only can remember how to spell. Must search before can watch, and must spell to search! Learned this the hard way. Always learning hard way, seems. During nap had bad dream about bears again. But not nice dead ones like in grandpa's whipping room. Don't like bears! Wish they wouldn't bother me anymore, awake or napping. Thank you!

Despite the much needed amusement afforded by this childlike journal entry, I still didn't know anything about the person who had written it, nor, more importantly, why it had been sent to me. The only possible clue was the initials "SS", which at first gave me a jolt. Could this possibly be Adolph Hitler's own personal diary? But then I realized that even if he was by some chance still alive, there was very little possibility he was an avid watcher of Gossip Girl. However, there are stranger things on Heaven and Earth, something something, Shakespeare…

I kept reading:

Dear Dairy,

Was supposed to meat some chick from State Department today, but then heard she not even hot, and probably just mad at me anyway, so told SS was sick again. Besides, Barron says he about to find most rare pokey-man. What pokey-man? I says. Why now? Had to take him all over in Groundforce 1 (what I call presidential limo, haha) just to find out. But still don't know! But do know that this pokey-man so rare that when he find (my son, whose I'm his father, with medical and everything) the color of leather in limo changed from gray to black, then back again. I said, what was that! But Barron pretend not to notice me. He always pretend not to hear what father (me) say. And sometimes tries to push me down stairs! Haha, kids never change. Never forget when tried to push own father down stairs first time, he reward me with first company. My own company! How should reward Barron? Who no seem to like work and companies. Rare pokey? But where? How? Must sleep now, dream of…well not your business! Haha. But please no dream of bears. Please!

Holy shit. I think I actually said that out loud. If I didn't know better, I'd think that maybe…But this next entry is what convinced me of what my eyes could scarcely believe:

Worried about Mel lately. Unusual distracted and or tense. Asked for ice-cream and she brought me mashed potatoes! Didn't say anything because also like potatoes, but still alarming! She think me don't notice, but me do notice! Just that usually don't care. But sometimes do care! Care about ice-cream 4 instance. Care about mean looks whenever I roam around White House without pajamas. Which, often! Followed Mel into oval office other day, but then she not there! But where go? Don't know. Would have asked her, but she not there to ask, which is why wanted to ask in first place! Being precedent hard! That all for today, think. So hungy and tired. No bears!

I sat there for a while, immobilized by a combination of excitement, disgust, and post-nasal drip. The dog, sensing I was upset about something, wandered over and licked himself, apparently for my benefit. Then, for an encore, he threw up on the diary. I scratched his ears and wiped up his vomit with one of Todd's tank tops.

Victoria's Secret

The Order of Athena was structured meticulously, with no single agent ever knowing enough to expose the master plan in the event that they were captured. Perhaps the only problem was that it was too effective. Nobody seemed to know the masterplan, other than HR presumably, who behind her familiar official designation was as unknowable as any human resources department anywhere. The orders were received old school to avoid a wire trail (though not quite as old school as they once were, when carrier falcons were the messengers of choice; not only were the falcons notoriously unreliable, they were also indiscreet, especially around election time, when falcon traffic got so dense that somebody alerted the FAA, who in turn alerted animal control, none of whom were eager to tangle with a bunch of goal-oriented falcons, many of whom being of questionable temperament), but the question remained: who was giving the orders? Who was HR?

Of course, throughout time there had been many incarnations of HR, some of whom were now known. Queen Victoria, for one. It was her idea to use the burgeoning lingerie industry as a conduit for clandestine operations. But I now had so many questions, and as she'd been dead for a long time it was doubtful that I could turn to Queen Victoria for answers. But where could I turn? Maverick was dead, most likely from not natural causes. There was apparently a mole of some kind working from within The Order, known only as The Hacker. Who was this mole? And how did they get so mole-ish?

The only place I could turn, HR, was the only place I couldn't turn, assuming HR had truly been compromised. The orange bastard was eating mashed potatoes like it was ice-cream, and was apparently spending most of his time driving around with his son looking for rare Pokémon. This last part was good news, actually. The more time he spent playing video games he didn't understand, the less time he would have to destroy the country and/or the multiverse as a whole.

It was a lot to put on the shoulders of a nice-ish girl from Alaska. The more I thought about it the clearer it became that there was only one person I could turn to. The person who had sent me the diary.

Codename: Melania

First thing I wish to say is I'm not actually talking like this. Don't think like this either, and certainly not my preferred prose style. But is necessary to stay in character. One thing about Melania, when she go in, she go in deep. Speaking of deep, I can now hear my husband, codename Goldilocks, splashing around in the tub. He enjoys bath time more than I've ever enjoyed anything. But if you think I'm holding that against him, you are correct.

He was splashing more than usual, now. I could tell from aggrieved timbre of his squealing that it was once again downhill ice-skating season on the Ocho, and that he had money riding. At least is more ethical than horse-racing, or dog-racing, or any of his other interests that for some reason all seem to involve hurting animals. The temptation to visit secret tunnel in oval office (offal orifice, Michelle once joked to me, but I did not and do not understand) was powerful. If only could think of way to getting past secret service (the SS initials always do me concern; in all likelihood is harmless coincidence, but you get enough seemingly harmless coincidences and line them up side by side, starts to look very much like firing squad).

But then I heard my name being called. Cried, more like.

Took me moment to realize, as have never fully gotten used to cover identity. Tried to ignore, but then realized couldn't hear splashing, which always bad sign. Was afraid that after bath he might wanting sex, and was trying to prepare self mentally.

Fortunately he was only choking on a chicken bone and had capsized in the bath again. Had to fish him out with elaborate pully system I invented (I studied to become engineer, once upon time). After I'd dislodged chicken bone and gotten him tucked into bed, his eyes red with tears and burst capillaries, he looked almost peaceful. Like large grotesque baby. He looked so almost peaceful that I almost felt sorry for him. Sorry that he was so poorly suited to living among humans, and sorry that our son was not actually his. Actually, not sorry for last thing. Eternally grateful for last thing.

He asked if I would get him bowl of ice-cream. But when I got ice-cream I realized that the Ambien I'd taken when thought he wanted sex had kicked in, and I'd accidentally gotten him a bowl of mashed potatoes. Oh well, I thought. Doubt he notice difference, anyway. Then, while crying in bathroom, I find what turns out to be diary. One more reason, I'm guessing, why he spend so long in bathroom all the time.

I think to myself, must take diary and send to someone.

Maybe to funny lady from television with scar on chin. Not sure why I did this, but must remember, had taken two Ambien. When sneaking diary out I see Donald sleeping with mouth open, muttering curses under his breath, hair flapping in breath-wind, mashed potatoes congealing on chin and neck. Sometimes when he sleeping I look at him and feel deep pity, but then remember what kind of person he is when not sleeping. When he's awake I only want to scream and rage against whatever monster gods created this world and then put it in the tiny pink hands of mutant like him. If only he could sleep forever, I might be able to forgive him for existing. But not while awake, and not with potatoes on face.

Sub Rosa

Once I'd decided to contact Melania, I realized that it wasn't going to be a simple matter. What I had to say to her wasn't for prying ears, and it certainly wasn't for her husband, who for all I knew was the enemy (I knew of course that he was *an* enemy, but I had strong doubts that someone of his limited mental resources could possibly be *the* enemy, especially after reading his diary). It was clear that the courier system of exchanging messages had been compromised. I remembered hearing about a website that had been used as a sort of dropbox for members, but that was before I'd been officially accepted, back when people still thought that electronic communication was more secure and reliable than physical couriers. Before it became clear that a reasonably gifted child could hack actual fucking election computers. And it was especially counter-intuitive to imagine that using the internet would be an effective counter-measure against an insurgent whose actual goddamn name was The Hacker, but there it was.

The website was called www.orderofathena.com. I'd seen it before, and beyond the boldness of hiding in plain sight, it hadn't impressed me much. And what I saw now didn't do a whole lot to change my opinion. On the surface it didn't seem to be anything more than a promotional page for some kind of book. And not a very detailed one at that. A landing page with the name of the book, and a bunch of quotations lauding said book, which frankly sounded made up. The only thing that interested me was a blank box at the bottom of the page with space for a few characters. I tried a few combinations but nothing happened.

Then something occurred to me. One of the images on the page was of a rose. *Sub Rosa*, a favorite phrase of my college professor, which meant something or other I couldn't recall. Except I knew that sub meant under. I tried clicking on the rose and nothing happened. I knew that even if I was able to access the dropbox there was very little chance of any of this working. If Melania was a member of The Order I had never heard anything about it. But it was policy that no single member ever be privy to a complete roster, so that didn't necessarily mean anything. This would be a lot easier if I could just show up at the White House, but I'd been considered persona non grata ever since the Easter party when an impromptu arm-wrestling match with Sarah Sanders had gotten out of hand, so to speak.

I was on the verge of giving up, maybe disappearing somewhere nice to live out whatever life was left to me. I highlighted the image almost by accident. Hidden within the image, when highlighted, was a series of numbers. I typed these numbers into the box and was taken to a second page. Now I'm cooking with gas, I thought. It was one of Todd's favorite phrases. One which used to annoy me because Todd doesn't cook, and what the hell does that even mean, anyway? But now something felt different, I realized. Maybe because I knew that whatever our lives together were, it was probably over. I tend to get a little wistful at the ends of things. Even unpleasant things. I remember crying because a scab I'd gotten on my knee had healed up. And that was just a couple months ago.

The second page was almost completely blank, except for another compass rose, in the center of which was another dialogue box with the two word prompt: name, message. What the hell, I thought. I typed in Melania's name and the words "Need to see you immediately, Sarah Palin." I had absolutely no confidence that this was going to work, but almost immediately I received a text message from a blank account. A time and an address. Was I going to voluntarily walk into a trap? Fuck it, I thought. Wouldn't be the first time, and my boots are still tapping.

The Unknown Man

The man hung up the phone and leaned back in his office chair, gazing affectionately at a framed photograph of Ronald Reagan he kept on his desk. The photo, a headshot from the former president's acting days, was autographed to a fan whose name he had never quite been able to make out. In any event, it wasn't his name. In fact, despite many years of fixation, he had never met the man. Though he'd once watched the former president from across a restaurant as he devoured an entire chicken. He'd spent the better part of an hour working up his nerve to go introduce himself, but at the last moment his courage failed him and instead he crawled out the bathroom window. He couldn't quite remember why he'd done that.

He'd been told by many people that he bore a striking resemblance to the handsome-ish republican hero. In fact, the resemblance was so striking that to look at himself in the mirror was almost like meeting him, and he would frequently have energetic conversations with himself.

The man had used many names in his life, but none of them meant anything to him. The only name he cared about was the one he couldn't use. Not yet. But soon he would reclaim his dynasty, his name, and all that it entailed. Known to the meaner spirited people he was required to do business with as Rudolph, on account of his nose, which was red and heavily veined from years of hard drinking. The man resented the name, and had compiled his own list of nicknames he would prefer, in a just world. In a just world he wouldn't have to drink all the time, and would have a cool nickname like Snake or Aladdin. But this world wasn't just, and he'd made it his life's work to change that fact. If only for himself.

Flexing one absurdly muscular bicep, he gazed at the motto he had tattooed there: *the world is not enough*. It was the family motto of James Bond, though he'd adopted it for himself. Nothing would ever be enough, not in this world. But this wasn't the only world. A fact known to very few, aside from himself. He knew many things that other people didn't know. Things they would laugh at him for, if he tried to tell them. They laughed at him anyway, despite the fact that he could do over twenty pullups. Twenty!

Just you wait, he thought. *Soon I'll do so many pullups that no one, man or woman, would dare laugh at me!* But first he had work to do, and a rotisserie chicken to eat, bones and all. Still staring at the photograph on his desk he did a few Kegels to fight against an increasingly embarrassing urinary problem, and repeated a promise he made several times a day. *Soon*, he said. *Very soon, now.*

Secret Cheeseburger Dreams

I didn't know what I was doing or who I was meeting (whom?), only that I was supposed to wait in the last changing room at the Victoria's Secret on Lexington, next door to what was considered the second worst pizza place in town. I was a few minutes early so I figured I'd look around a little. There was a buy one get one sale on bras and I even picked up a teddy that nobody would ever see or appreciate.

I'd apparently overstayed my welcome in the dressing room because soon there was a loud and insistent knocking on the door. Just when I thought they were going to break the door down and haul me out of there, the rear wall of the dressing room opened and Melania was there. She took me back through a secret passageway into a long hall.

"Next to the pizza place." I said. "Wow, so those conspiracy idiots were actually almost onto something?"

"Much closer than anyone could've imagined."

"Well, you know what they say about blind dogs…"

"No, I don't. We don't have any such proverb in Bulgaria."

"It must be an Alaska thing. They're always on about blind dogs. Anyway, it means that even idiots are right every now and then."

"This is true." Melania nodded in agreement. "Last night Donald tells me he's worried about new mole on his scrotum. I'm thinking, there's no way he would be knowing about this mole, even if is there. How would he know? Tell me this! But sure enough, is there. Big mole. Angry mole. Looking very cancerous. I tell him, don't even worry about it, is merely piece of chocolate. So he keeps licking his finger and trying to rub off chocolate, which is actually mole. Rubbing and licking, rubbing and licking! And mole is getting angrier! Eventually he broke the skin and I had to superglue wound. Supergluing old man's balls not what I signed up for."

"Tell me about it. Being unappreciated for who you are, and hated for who you're not is a brutal combination."

"Very brutal combination. Add old man's torn ballsack and even worse combination."

I had to agree, choking back a mixture of tears and vomit.

"And he didn't even seem surprised that he would have a piece of chocolate stuck to his balls!"

"What even happens if you rupture a cancerous mole, anyway?"

"Don't know." She shrugged. "Guess will find out."

"Well at least there's something to look forward to in this godforsaken Berenstain timeline."

"And if cancer-mole takes too long, can always bonk him on the head. Almost positive his fontanelle never closed up."

"Good to know," I nodded. "By the way, you don't have to keep up with the accent and everything when it's just the two of us."

"Is habitual now. I like, even. Very liberating. You should give try."

"I have my own version, *doncha know*."

"Da, have noticed. Charming in its way."

"Thank you. B-t-dubs, are you sure it's okay to just stroll into the oval office like this?"

"Is no problem. Donald just ate three cheeseburgers, he won't notice anything."

"He won't think it's weird that Sarah Palin walks into the room from behind a painting?"

"I'm telling you, three. Doubles. He wouldn't notice if you peed on the couch. Which, if you're interested, there could be some money in it for you."

"How much? Nevermind, I already have more money than Sarah Palin would know what to do with. I just can't spend it on anything nice without blowing my cover.

Seriously though, there's only so much cocaine, white wine, and snowmobiling a girl can take before she starts to lose her way."

"Yes, we also have this proverb in Bulgaria."

"It's not really a proverb, but nevermind that."

We reached the end of the dimly lit tunnel. There was a small door, heavily reinforced.

"Waiting here one second," Melania said, using a small, ornate key to unlock the door. Momentarily disappearing into what I could see was the oval office. I took a deep, involuntary breath, remembering how close I'd come to occupying it.

Sure, it wasn't like I was actually a politician pursuing the nation's highest office, and I'd only gotten as far as I did because of and in service to The Order, but still, it stung a bit. Power is, well, a powerful thing. Looking back, I realized it was almost exactly ten years earlier. Is that when things had gone wrong? I knew that they'd gone wrong for me, anyway. God, the insane things I'd said in interviews, some of them on live television! I couldn't remember much from that time—for whatever reason, don't worry about it—but that was probably for the best. I never understood what had gone wrong. Of course, if we had won that would mean that Obama wouldn't have become president, which would have been worse than The Order being temporarily derailed.

Melania stepped back into the tunnel, shaking her head.

"No good." She said. "Goldilocks asleep on couch."

"I see," I squinted, wondering if the pee-pee offer was still on the table. "Goldilocks asleep on the couch. Let's hope the bears get home in time."

"Shhhh!" Melania gasped, pressing a well-lacquered fingernail against my lips, her eyes suddenly wide. "Never, ever, mention anything about bears around Goldilocks. Last time someone talked to him about bears he tore his shirt off and nearly jumped off the balcony."

"What a missed opportunity." I said. "What's his deal?"

"Not sure. Can't be discussing for obvious reasons. Something that happened to him when little boy."

"Fair enough. Look, the reason I contacted you is I… something weird is going on, and I don't know what to do or who to talk to. I wasn't even sure I could talk to you, but I guess the fact that you got my message means you're okay."

"True. Member since I was teenage girl. Models have much access to people and places others don't."

"Yeah, they made a movie about that. And I'm pretty

sure they got sued, so let's not discuss it anymore."

"Anyway, must confess, when I send you diary, thought was sending to Tina Fey."

"I don't understand…"

"Ambien."

"Oh. That makes sense."

"But then I check with HR and turns out you also member. Must say, was bit surprised."

"That makes two of us. But I have to ask, why? Beyond the obvious comedic value of the diary, which so far I've enjoyed immensely, what is it that I was supposed to get from it?"

"There are things in it. Strange things, even for him. Might have to do with same weirdness you're talking. And there's something else." She handed me a folded sheaf of printed pages. The front page was covered in drawings of penises, some of them rather exquisite in their detail. There also seemed to be a lot of what was either congealed blood or ketchup. I prayed for the latter.

"I had no idea Donald could draw like that."

Melania frowned. "No, the drawings are definitely Mike. The ketchup is Donald's though."

What could be important enough to steal from the desk of the president, but unimportant enough to draw dicks on and use as a napkin? And when would I learn to stop asking questions about things that don't make sense? Nothing makes sense, not anymore.

"Need you to take diary, and this, to HR. Sending messages one thing, but no way can deliver this."

She didn't know about HR.

"HR is compromised. I'm almost sure of it."

"I was afraid of that, when got message from old website. Is there anything we can do?"

"There might be." I said.

Queen of Thorns

I was still in my first year of college (first year back in Idaho, anyway, studying in Hawaii hadn't been as productive as my parents had hoped) when they came to recruit me. I had just finished supergluing all of my dormmate, Lucy's bras and underwear to the outside wall of our common area when I got thirsty and went looking for a jug of not-quite-rancid Chablis I'd hidden in a shrub somewhere.

I wasn't having much luck finding the wine, but I did find a tiny and odd looking woman crouched among a grove of dying roses. At first I thought she was stuck there in the thorns and I pretended not to notice her out of fear that she might want my help getting out. But there was something about her. I was especially struck by her ability to remain dignified while trapped in a shrub. She was dressed in what I at first mistook for a garbage bag. Her shoes were vaguely orthopedic. Her name, I eventually learned, was Ruth. And though you probably know her as your favorite supreme court justice, I'll always think of her as the Queen of Thorns.

I asked her what she was doing there (trying to steal my wine, I assumed) and was surprised to hear that she was looking for me. I told her everyone knew where to find me and that it would've been easier just to ask. She said she had asked, and that she was informed the best place to look was in the bushes. And that while searching the bushes she found a jug of wine.

Fair enough.

As I tried to help her out of the thorns she explained that there would come a time when the full scope of my destiny would become known and that I should try not to fuck up my life too bad in the meantime. She said that despite my rough exterior, and questionable interior, she believed in me. The problem with having someone believe in you is that now you actually have to do something. No more slinking around in existential shadows, contenting yourself with runner-up status in local beauty pageants and the occasional hazing ritual. Which, if I'm being honest, I miss almost as much as I miss the smooth, burnished sheen of my own teenage thighs.

By the time I eventually graduated from college I'd pretty much forgotten about the whole episode, or had at least convinced myself it was some kind of drunken hallucination. I worked for several years in various jobs, none of which ever gave me the power I wanted and needed, until one day I was walking down the street and a black limousine pulled up next to me. I was ready to launch my smoothie in the face of whatever asshole was trying to ruin my day, when the window lowered. It was her, the Queen of Thorns.

I was taken to a secret room in the basement of the library, and it was there that I finally learned the truth about the world. A truth that has both nurtured and haunted me ever since.

"You have no idea how much careful plotting it takes just to keep the world turning." She told me. I don't think she meant literally.

She told me about the last time The Order had lost control, back in 1984. Between campaigning and taking pictures of himself in the bathroom mirror, Reagan forgot about the part where he was supposed to be a caretaker for the country and its diverse and needy population. And Nancy didn't do her job either, which was to make sure that the president did his. Instead she was popping pills and endlessly knitting doilies. So many doilies. She knitted so many that she lost her puppy under a pile of them and didn't find him until H.W. moved into the Whitehouse and had the knitting room excavated.

They found the remains of two dogs, a handful of cats, and a child no one had ever even known about. The animals were a lost cause, but Barbara B. was able to resuscitate the kid using some kind of sorcery she'd apparently learned from Aleister Crowley. George Sr. didn't like the idea of her using magic in the house (especially didn't like her keeping so many potions and powders around where W. could get his hands on them). Saving the life of a previously unknown Reagan child would have made great press, if they'd been allowed to talk about it. But of course, they weren't. The Reagan kid was sent to live with distant relatives in South Africa, but disappeared shortly after his thirteenth birthday. Nobody had ever seen or heard from his since.

Except, I now speculated, Maverick. And it had potentially cost him his life.

At first I thought there had to be some kind of mistake. I wasn't really all that ambitious. All I wanted was to be Governor of some big and beautiful but ultimately useless non-contiguous state, and to spend my time bullying people about things I didn't really care about. But they really sold it to me. Especially the part where I already knew too much and that if I said no it'd be game over for old Sarah P.

My first job was that I had to kill Mr. O'Malley, the creepy crossing guard who apparently liked kids more than you'd think from the lackadaisical way he directed them into oncoming traffic. Well I'd already been planning on killing him, so I figured what the hell. The only problem was that I was supposed to do it in a lowkey manner that wasn't my style at all. I snuck into his house (redacted)…

Once I proved my value they started the ball rolling on my eventual move to the Governor's house in Alaska, which I wasn't too keen on until they pointed out that it was literally the only state that met my requirements. Not only would the job put me above suspicion with regards to the numerous targets I'd be eliminating, but the rigorous travel schedule made things pretty convenient. I was worried that people would recognize me when I was acting in my true but secret capacity, but it turns out that famous people have to work pretty hard to get recognized. If Beyoncé walked around by herself without makeup, no one would say anything to her (except for the dickholes whose job it apparently is to go around saying stupid shit to women in public).

Now the time had come for me to be truly tested, and I was pretty sure I didn't have the goods. I didn't want the burden, and would gladly have passed it off to someone else. But with all normal lines of communication compromised, there was nobody else. My only option left was to call a phone number. A number that was strictly for the most apocalyptic emergencies. Taking a deep breath, I punched in the numbers. I felt my heart beating rapidly as I listened to the ringing, part of me not convinced anyone would pick up, and hoping no one would. But then the line clicked and I heard the sound of breathing. Fine, cultured breathing.

"I'd hoped to never receive this call." Oprah said.

"I'd hoped to never make it." I replied. "Actually, that's not true. I've been wanting to make this call for a long time. Just not under these circumstances. I was thinking more like a spa day, or maybe even a beach vacation or something."

"That sounds nice, actually. But it's clearly not why you're calling. There's somebody you need to see. You have to find HR. I'm sending you a set of coordinates, but I'm warning you, if you let them get out it could mean the end of everything."

"Isn't there anything else you can tell me? I feel like I'm out in the cold. Well, I *am* out in the cold, but you know what I mean. Todd's going to sober up at some point. Maybe. If he does he might start asking questions. He's never shown much curiosity before, but I've learned to expect the unexpected. If he does ask questions, I won't know what to tell him. I'm starting to feel like this is all a lot bigger than a presidential election. Which sounds like a crazy thing to say."

"This is much bigger than a presidential election." Oprah sighed. "Just follow the numbers. Find HR.

The first thing I did was look up the upstate New York coordinates on Google Earth. But there was nothing there. Just a vast forest, no buildings of any kind. But that didn't necessarily mean anything. There were many locations that were intentionally invisible to the all-seeing eye of technology. Such as certain military bases, and the Bush family compound in Kennebunkport, Maine. To be sure I'd have to go there in person.

The League of Extraordinarily Lonely Gentlemen

It turns out I'm not much of an orienteer. I wish I could say I've just gotten too used to the conveniences of technology and have forgotten how to read a map, follow coordinates, but the truth is I was never good at it even back before there was any such thing as cell phones and the internet. And I was even worse now. I felt like I'd reached Point Nemo—the farthest place from land, closer to the International Space Station than another living person. Obviously none of that was true, but you know what I mean.

After fruitlessly stumbling around in the woods some more, my pants chafing, my dogs barking, my hair reaching epic levels of frizz, I decided that I was going to require sustenance to continue.

By some miracle I was able to find my way back to my rental car, this time a somewhat respectable Mercury Cougar, the connotations of which I chose to ignore. After circling my way back to the interstate, I came across one of those little towns that is so insignificant it hardly warrants a name. A town whose crowning achievement was the fact that they boasted a Denny's. I parked on the street and looked around for a meter to feed quarters to, but there wasn't one. Even Wasilla has parking meters these days. But it's a silly thing to complain about, I guess, not getting to constantly pay money for the privilege of merely existing.

There were only a couple other people inside the Denny's, one of whom was hunched over a laptop working on what—judging from the ferocity of his typing—he must've thought was a masterpiece. Yet another addition to the culture's already bloated collection of mediocre male-gaze literature. I guess it's a cliché to refer to people typing "furiously", but in his case it was the literal truth. His fingers struck the keys with such percussive intensity I was afraid he might break them clean off. He was wearing one of those weird hats that Sherlock Holmes wore—a deerstalker I think it's called, though I have no idea why I know that.

I briefly tried to look over his shoulder, but he noticed me immediately and hid what he was working on, the way kids used to hide their quizzes so I couldn't cheat off of them. Who's around to protect people like that? We're supposed to help the vulnerable, and who's more vulnerable than a middle aged man who thinks his words are worth spying on? I was reminded of a group of old men that used to hang out all day at the diner when I was in high school. We called them the League of Extraordinarily

Lonely Gentlemen, which I guess sounds kind of mean, in retrospect. Not to mention, the movie referenced by that derisive moniker didn't actually come out until the late nineties, so I wasn't a teenager, or even in my twenties anymore.

I considered slipping some poison in his coffee, just to put him out of his misery. But then my eggs and toast arrived. As if he'd been waiting for that moment, the only other patron of the Denny's swaggered over to my booth, sipping some kind of brown soda with a straw. Something about him seemed out of place. His clothes a little too neat, his muscles a little too developed, his teeth a little too still in his mouth. Actually, he looked a bit like a youngish Ronald Reagan. An alarm went off in my head, and I prepared myself for whatever the coming moments might bring.

"You're not from around here," he said, more a statement of fact than a question.

"What makes you say that?"

"Because I'm not either." He said, helping himself to the seat opposite me. "We can smell our own, maybe. Let me guess, you're some kind of attorney. Financial I'd say. Got tired of the city and figured you'd move upstate, get ahead of the rush."

"How'd you know?"

"Because I had the same thought. Problem is, we're a little *too* ahead of the rush. That's always been my problem, thinking too far ahead. You know," he said, sipping through his straw. "I had the idea for Instagram back when everyone else still thought the internet would be a passing trend."

"So what happened?"

"Blew my investor's money on other things. Drugs mostly. And hookers. And drugs for the hookers. It happens that my investor was also my wife, so she took the whole thing pretty personally. Had to spend a few months in Otisville. Started reading a lot. By the time I got out, I knew I couldn't hack the city anymore. Fortunately, I still had enough cash tucked away here and there to buy a spread, build a house. I didn't build it personally, of course."

"So I guess that about brings us up to date." I said, taking a bite of my already cold eggs, sipping some lukewarm coffee.

"You look familiar to me." He squinted. "Do you know Deb at Barney's?"

I told him I did not.

"That's the problem with this place. I got here too soon.

In a few years it'll be the new Jackson Hole, without the skiing of course, but for now it's just about impossible to find anyone worth talking to, let alone sharing day-drinks in the hot tub."

"I'm sorry to hear that." I told him, looking around for the waitress.

"I have a hot tub, is what I'm getting at."

"I'm really happy for you," I said. "And maybe if my life went totally to shit and I had to choose between your hot tub and say, bathing in sulphuric acid, there's a fifty-fifty shot I'd choose your hot tub. But there's also a chance I'd end up karate chopping your neck for what you did to your, obviously ex, wife."

"It didn't even happen to you, why take it so personally?"

"Every woman is a conduit for all the grievances of all women throughout history."

"Look, I think you've got me all wrong. I write poetry for godsake."

"Poetry is a dying insect," I told him, scooping up the last of my eggs with a piece of toast and washing it down with shitty coffee. "And I have no time for men who drink through straws."

When I got back out to the car I noticed another restaurant across the street I hadn't seen the first time. A

Mexican place, if I was to believe the neon sombrero in the window. Had I actually failed to notice it the first time, I wondered, or had it not been there? And more importantly, what was Mexican food like in upstate New York? I had a morbid curiosity to find out, but my appetite—while not exactly satisfied—was more or less expunged from record. I figured I'd give it a try the next time I got lost in the woods.

The Cabin in the Woods

After checking my information again, I went back to the same place I'd been before, walked the same trails, suffered the same but now aggravated chafing. Except this time I found a cabin, which I'm almost positive hadn't been there before. Crouching in the tree line I watched for activity, rubbing my calves and cursing this so-called Denny and his legacy of mediocrity.

The cabin was empty, and showed no signs of recent habitation. I thought maybe my information was bad after all. I'd followed the coordinates exactly, and this was the only manmade structure within a square mile. Dropping myself onto a musty but suspiciously stylish divan, raising a cloud of dust, I stared at the ceiling and laid out the pieces of information inside my head like playing cards. Was this another of the Hacker's games? And if so, what was the point? Was there a point? I couldn't help but feel I'd gotten caught up in a child's game, whose nebulous rules changed according to invisible whims.

Finally, there was nothing else to do but uncork my emergency rosé. Which soon led to lighting up my emergency cigarette, which was laced with just enough hash to take the edge off without compromising my tradecraft.

Exhaling a dense cloud, feeling almost good for a change, I noticed the smoke move in an unusual way. Almost as if blown by a breeze, which should've been impossible in this dank and fetid chamber, which had eastern facing windows, terrible airflow, and suffered from a variety of other examples of poor Feng Shui.

Extinguishing the spliff, I made a second and more thorough search of the mostly empty bookshelves behind me. For a second time my search produced nothing but a rather extensive collection of kid's books. Berenstein Bears. Stein!

I reached for one of the volumes but was distracted by a framed photograph of Maya Angelou. I'd noticed it before, but this time I wiped the dust off with my sleeve. Standing next to the Nobel laureate was none other than Hillary, the true and rightful president. I felt a surge of energy. Relighting the emergency cigarette, which let's face it was basically a joint, I blew smoke along the wall until I found the source of the breeze under another framed photograph, this one of Nelson Mandela in his first public appearance after being released from prison. I tried to remove the photo from the wall but it was firmly attached. I pushed it in all directions until finally it gave and I heard a low groaning sound from within the wall, and the floor fell out from under me.

I couldn't tell how far I fell, but it was enough to knock the wind out of me—along with an acrid lungful of smoke—when I hit solid ground. Climbing to my feet, I felt along a wall through the darkness, afraid of falling again. I was sick to death of falling all the time. The air got cold and damp and it became difficult to breath, so I reluctantly quit smoking the joint. Finally, a light appeared ahead of me. Dim but undeniable. But before I could reach the source of the light a voice stopped me and my chest went cold and I nearly shit myself, which would've been a disaster considering I hadn't brought a change of clothes.

"I've been expecting you." The voice said. "Nice Shahtoosh."

"Uh, thank you?"

"Come closer." The voice beckoned. It was a familiar voice.

"Who are you?"

A figure stepped into the light at the end of the tunnel. A woman. Her Chanel pantsuit even smarter and more finely tailored than I would've thought possible.

"Madam President?"

"Just call me HR." Hillary Rodham said. "And now, if you could be so kind, how about some of that reefer I smelled. One of the only benefits of losing the election is that I can smoke all the weed I want. I have to, in fact, or I'd probably lose my mind."

"I guess it's been pretty tough on you, huh."

"The horror, Sarah, the horror."

I handed her the joint and a lighter, but just as she was about to get down to business some kind of alarm sounded.

"Shit," she sighed, handing me back my wares and taking a seat in front of a bank of monitors from where we could see footage of virtually every square inch of the property surrounding her hidden compound. On one screen there was some kind of large rodent looking creature, maybe a weasel?

"False alarm?" I said hopefully.

"Look again."

I gazed at the screens but saw nothing. But then I did. It was a man, dressed in some kind of uniform.

"You expecting a plumber?"

She shook her head. Then I saw the large and brutal looking weapon he was carrying. It was hard to tell from the small image, but I it looked like a combat ready AR-15, with an extended magazine and rail-mounted laser scope. Then I saw his face and it hit me. The timing couldn't be a coincidence. Whoever he really was, I had led him from the diner directly to HR.

"Let me take care of this." I said, cracking my knuckles. Hillary didn't argue. "Is there any other way outside?" I asked. "Other than the hole I fell through?"

"Through here." She said, showing me to a discrete looking door. "There's a tunnel, about twenty yards long. At the end there's another door that'll put you about here." She pointed at a spot on one of the screens. "You should be able to come up behind him. But be careful, he doesn't seem like he's here for fun. Are you armed?"

"Sure am." I said. Finally, carrying around my special polymer pistol will have been worth it. I reached for my bag, but it wasn't there. "Shit."

"Is that good shit or bad shit?"

"Bad shit." I said. I'd left my bag on the sofa up in the main room of the cabin. The interloper was already too close to the door and I wouldn't have time to climb back up there. "Looks like I'm going to have to do this *au natural.*"

"Then you'd better hurry. Once he gets inside it's going to be a lot harder to surprise him, and without a weapon surprise is pretty much all we've got."

"What about that gaping hole in the floor that I fell

through? Don't you think he might see that?"

"Don't worry about that, it closed up behind you. Now go, for godsake. Hold on." She hugged me. "For luck." She smelled so nice I almost forgot what I was doing. I always assumed she smelled better than anyone on Earth, and I was right.

"Wow." I said.

"I know." She winked.

The tunnel felt longer than twenty yards. I couldn't see where I was going and that made it feel even longer. My forehead started sweating and my mascara stung my eyes. I can only imagine what I looked like. Finally, I reached the end of the tunnel and slowly opened the door. Suddenly I was facing the cabin from the front. I saw the man looking through the window. A little careless, I thought. Maybe this wouldn't be as hard as I'd thought.

The ground was littered with small twigs and I had to be careful not to step on any. If he saw me before I got to him I'd be roasted. As quickly as I could without making any noise I approached him, ready to tackle him if necessary. I knew I could cover the last few yards in a dash, so once I was within range I got ready. He was still looking at the window.

Something felt wrong in my stomach. It was too

easy. Only an amateur would make it this easy, and they (whoever they were) would never send an amateur after HR. Then in a sickening moment of shock I realized what was wrong. He wasn't looking in the window at all. He was looking *at* the window. At his reflection, and at mine. He'd been watching me the whole time. I made my move anyway because it was too late for anything else. As I was diving for him he turned and cracked me across the head with the butt of his rifle. I saw a bright flash inside my head, and then nothing.

Mole Hunt

I woke up with what I at first assumed was a brutal hangover. I rolled over in bed and called out to Todd to cook up some bacon and fetch me a Mexi-Coke, the combination of which is the best hangover cure I've ever discovered. But I wasn't in bed, and Todd was thousands of miles away, doing who knows what. And for better or worse, I wasn't even hungover. I did however have an egg sized welt on my head and a vaguely copperish taste in my mouth.

"What happened?"

"You failed, is what." Hillary said.

Then I remembered what had happened, along with some other stuff I'd forgotten, like what color my underwear were and the combination to my locker in high school. Getting hit on the head is a weird trip.

"Sorry." I said.

"Don't worry about it." She said. "Well, *do* worry about it. But, like, don't worry about it, if you know what I mean."

I had no idea what she meant.

"Hey you two, shut up." A man's voice said. We were in what must've been a bedroom in the unused ground level portion of the cabin. Hillary was handcuffed to a radiator. Actually we both were, it turned out. I could hear the man talking to someone in the other room. But I couldn't hear the other person so he must've been on the phone. Craning my neck as far as I could without risking a spinal injury, I tried to hear what he was saying, but either I was still suffering side effects from the whole getting hit in the head thing, or he was too far away, because I could've sworn he said something about enchiladas.

"Man," Hillary said. "I could really go for some enchiladas. You hungry?"

"Yes, actually." I admitted. "But I also wouldn't mind some freedom and safety."

"Overrated." She shook her head. "The safety part, anyway. And it doesn't exist either way, so let's focus on enchiladas."

"Hey!" The man barked, poking his head in the door. "What'd I tell you?" We looked at each other, but he betrayed no indication that he'd ever seen me before.

"Are you an actor or something?" I asked him.

"I'm an executioner If you don't stop talking." He growled, withdrawing back to the other room, but then quickly stepping back in. "Why? Do you think I could be?"

"I mean, yeah." I said. "You certainly have the look, anyway."

"Really? Do you know anybody who might represent me?"

"I might," Hillary said. "If we could work out some kind of quid pro quo. What were you saying about enchiladas?"

"Listen." He said. "I have to go get the van. You two stay here and be good, and maybe I won't kill you."

"Get the van?"

"I couldn't very well pull up to the house, could I? But I also can't kidnap two women on foot, so yes, I have to get the van."

"If you bring us something to eat, maybe I can make some calls about getting you representation."

"Goddamnit." The man said, appearing to consider the offer. "I'll think about it."

"That's all I ask." Hillary said.

I heard his footsteps fade and then the door close.

"So," she said, once we were sure he'd gone. "You still have that joint?"

I did.

"What've you been listening to?" Hillary asked, holding the smoke in. "I know I'm a little late to the game but I recently got into Kate Bush. Very cool stuff. I didn't have much time to do anything fun in the nineties, or eighties for that matter. I've been trying to catch up. Have you ever heard of Borat? My wife, my wife."

"I can only imagine that this whole time/space paradox is eating into your free time. I know I haven't even cranked up a snowmobile for months."

"So," she said, looking me in the eyes, suddenly more serious than before. "You know about the paradox?"

I nodded. "At first I just noticed some weird things, like the airplane seats changing color, and the fact that my teenage daughter didn't have any kids of her own. And the fact that my husband was coming home at a reasonable hour and wearing clean shirts. I thought he was just getting uppity, but then the evidence became overwhelming when I saw that my favorite books had different names."

"Goddamn Berenstain, eh?"

"Fucking Berenstain. However, I wasn't really a hundred percent about it until just now. Sarah Palin might have some weird delusions about parallel universes, but not Hillary Rodham. If Hillary Rodham believes it, it must be true. And honestly, it makes a lot more sense than Todd wearing clean shirts for no reason."

I told her about the diary I'd gotten in the mail—which

had apparently not been intended for me at all—and my meeting with Melania.

"Ah, the old Victoria's Secret." Hillary smiled. "In plain sight is always the best place to hide," she said. I glanced around her secretive cabin. "Unless you're me, of course. By the way, you don't happen to have the diary with you? I'd love to take a look at it."

"It's in my bag." I said. "In the other room." *Along with my pistol.*

"Sonofabitch."

I tried to ask how she'd gotten involved with The Order, but she was reticent about details.

"All realms of human activity are given to entropy. But perhaps none more so than politics. The Order of Athena exists to keep the political realm in check, and to pick up the pieces when they inevitably go to shit. But more than that, we keep all the human project in check. Chaos and suffering are life's neutral gears, and if you think things are chaotic now, try to imagine the world without us. I assure you, it is not possible. At least not until now. Something has changed."

"The paradox?"

"Exactly. The only hope we have is to discover the cause, and to reverse it. If that's even possible."

"It might not be?"

"We're off the known map here. Nothing is certain. But we have to try. Call it noblesse-obligé. You're familiar with the term?"

I was of course familiar with the term, but since I was the product of dense, hirsute people who didn't know the difference between a button and a boutonnière, in our case the more appropriate phrase would be something like: no-bless, no-bligé.

As she spoke I was reminded of my professor in college and her ecstatic rants about purity and authenticity, or some such shit. I remembered the pain in her eyes when we failed to join her mystical reveries, and the way she would nervously rearrange all the objects on her lectern, her lip quivering. The way we felt was that the world was already fucked up when we got here, and it never occurred to us that it could be any other way. And I was always too hungover to get anything she was talking about anyway. Drinking beer and gluing other people's underwear to the wall seemed authentic enough for my tastes. None of that changed until I was recruited into The Order. Not that the world was suddenly okay, but at least it didn't feel dead anymore, and neither did I.

The difference was that I was ready now. Ready to listen.

And I felt in her words some kind of inner momentum that made me believe that it was actually possible to do something good in this world. It was a heady, unusual feeling, and only partially because of the joint we'd just smoked.

I'm pretty sure.

For once I'd encountered someone with a superior mind with whom I was not only willing, but eager, to join on whatever kind of journey might transpire. Unfortunately, this beautiful moment was somewhat mitigated by the fact that we'd been taken hostage and would probably be killed. I wasn't too keen on that part of the situation.

"Hillary," I said. "May I call you Hillary?"

"You bet."

"What about Hill?"

"We're not there yet."

"Fair enough. I think it's safe to say that we find ourselves in what amounts to one hell of a jam. I don't suppose you have any idea how to get out of it? I realize it's unfair of me to ask, considering it's basically my fault."

"Getting out of the jam is no sweat. You think he's the first asshole to come poking around my woods? The trick is to stay in the jam long enough to get information out of him, without him realizing we've actually been in control the whole time. Or at least I have. No offense."

"And how do we do that?"

"Well, I suppose you've noticed that you seem to have a certain effect on men." She said, looking at my face, my smeared and sweaty makeup. She winced a little. "Especially men who, and there's no kind way to say this, men with somewhat below average intelligence."

I started to argue, but then thought about Todd, and Levi, and my friend's brother, and boyfriend, and dad…

"Yeah, I see what you mean."

"There's one other thing I should mention. This jam, as you put it, isn't entirely your fault."

"How do you mean?"

"Well, surely you don't think Oprah would've given you my location without my permission?"

"I still don't understand." I confessed. "Let's pretend for the sake of this conversation that I also have somewhat below average intelligence."

"I got reliable intel that there was an unknown agent working against us, so I came up here to lay low. Though to be honest I'd already been spending a fair amount of time here these last couple years. Anyway, once it became clear to me that our lines of communication had been compromised it led me to suspect a mole."

"And you thought I was the mole?"

"As much as I hate to imagine any of my sisters working against us, it would be naïve not to consider it a possibility."

"You knew I'd be followed here."

"I considered it a strong possibility. The good news is that I trust you, Sarah. Not only that, I think I like you."

"You like me?"

"You seem surprised. Am I the first person to tell you that?"

"That's neither here nor there." I said. I could hear what sounded like a van pulling up in front of the cabin. "So, if this was all a test, does that mean he's just a part of your plan? Does he work for you?"

"No," she shook her head. "That particular threat is very real. However, I think I can figure something out. Just follow my lead. And whether or not you want to show any nipple is entirely up to you."

"Nipple?"

"Hey!" The man shouted. "What in God's name are you talking about now?"

"She needs to use the bathroom." Hillary said.

"Christ," the man sighed. "I could've been an optometrist…"

Fishing in his pocket for the key to the handcuffs, he didn't see that Hillary had already picked the lock and freed herself. As he reached down to uncuff us he saw what she'd done, but too late. Reaching up with a surprisingly muscular arm, Hillary got him in a headlock, and in one smooth motion twisted. I heard a sickening crunch of bone and the man's body went limp.

"Magic camp." Hillary said triumphantly. "Fifth grade."

"You learned to break necks in fifth grade magic camp?"

"I learned to pick locks." She frowned. "Sarah, please try to keep up with me."

Enchilada Diaries

As it turned out, the now deceased mercenary in the other room had been true to his word. At least on the food front. A bag containing four entrées was on the kitchen table. As we ate we took turns reading Goldilocks's diary entries:

Dear Diary,

had lunch with Tony Soprano. Thought he was my cousin Jeffery until bill came and I paid it. Would never pay for lunch with family, so must've been Tony! Tore up bill before waiter could get greasy Greek fingers on it. Must maintain market value of signature in case people discover don't know what am doing, and have to find new way to ~~steal~~ earn money. Sad again today.

Dear Diary,

just found out favorite reality show is in Japanese and never noticed. How will find out what happens with Shion and Tsubasa? Dark days in White House! Found more poison filled envelopes in Barron's desk while looking for crayon sharpener. Why do they always go after kids? Too afraid of me and my big hands, I bet. Also lost entire rotisserie chicken on way to bathroom. How am I supposed to take bath w/o chicken? Will my enemies stop at nothing? Will I ever feel clean again?

Dear Diary,

got in fight with strange woman I caught stealing my undershirts. She fought hard but I got a few good licks in. Turns out was Mel whole time! Never saw her without makeup before. All is okay now, but she says if I ever lick her again she'll call her dad. Never met him, but imagine him big and hairy. Scary! Would rather die than touch another man's hair. Except for man whose hair I put on my head. He's decent guy, whoever he is. Caught glimpse of self in mirror while fighting wife, almost got boner. Feel hopeful for future!

Dear Diary,

Colbert making fun of me again. Would have him killed but somebody hid my phone. Looked everywhere except drawer where Mel keeps female stuff. If phone is in this drawer it might as well be gone, because would sooner die. How do you get a new phone? Can't remember, or never knew. Wish someone would answer these questions, but they can't because this is my own super top secret personal diary, and if somebody read it I would die. But first I would have them killed, if I could find my phone. Hard to be a grownup!

"As much as I'm enjoying these diary entries," Hillary said, swallowing a forkful of pulled chicken, "I can't say that I'm finding much in them that I would consider especially helpful."

"I see what you mean."

"Not to mention it's got something gross all over it."

"My dog threw up on it."

"Good dog. Did she explain why exactly she sent it to you?"

"Well, she meant to send it to Tina Fey, actually. And her answer to both questions was 'Ambien'."

"Oh. Yeah, that makes sense. By the way, should we split his lunch? I don't think it's going to do him much good, and neck-breaking always gives me a killer appetite."

"You take it," I said, searching my purse for the roll of antacids. "I'm feeling a little queasy. Besides, I think there are four servings in there."

"Four?" She asked. "I wonder…"

"Did you happen to notice if the man you just killed had a pistol on him?"

"I would imagine he did, why?"

"Mine is gone, along with some other documents. And my goddamn Tums."

"Looking for these?" A man's voice said. I looked up and thought maybe I'd put too much hash into the spliff, because it was the same man whose neck Hillary had just snapped. "Good to see you again." He winked at me. "Bet you'd rather be in a hot tub about now?"

He was pointing a gun at me.

My gun.

And he was waving around antacids.

My antacids.

Keeping the gun on us, the man edged towards the bedroom and saw his doppelganger lying in a heap on the floor. I expected him to react violently when he saw what we'd done. But he didn't.

"Excellent." He said. "That's very convenient for me, thank you. Here's a little reward." He tossed me what was left of the roll of Tums.

"Hey," Hillary protested. "I broke his neck, I should get the Tums."

"They're my goddamn Tums." I said. "And they always were."

"Nevermind the Tums!" The man snapped. "Now, onto more important things." With one hand he reached for the bag on the table, then stopped. "Okay, so clearly the handcuffs aren't going to work. Let's see. How about, you two get on the couch. I'll sit here and eat my lunch, and if either of you moves I'll blow your brains out. Believe it. I don't need either one of you, and even if I did, I know where to get more." He said, nodding at his deceased double. "Speaking of which, I was going to kill him myself after lunch, but since you did it for me that means I get to eat his share too."

"Uh," Hillary said. "About that…"

"You already ate everything?" The man roared, throwing the empty bag across the room. "You're going to regret that."

"Believe me," Hillary said, clutching her stomach. "I already do. And as far as that goes, I'm going to need the facilities. And maybe a couple of those."

I growled and tossed her the antacids.

"Alright," the man sighed, apparently faint from hunger. "Move. And the door stays open."

"You sure about that?" Hillary frowned.

The man thought about it. "Okay, the door stays closed, fan on, but if you try anything funny, like say crawl out of the window, your friend here will suffer for it."

"She's fully prepared to give her life for our cause, as am I."

"Whoa, slow down a little." I said, and turned to the man. "She doesn't know what she's talking about."

"Oh, there's another thing." Hillary said. "The plumbing doesn't work up here."

"You really expect me to believe that Hillary Clinton is

living in a cabin in the woods with no plumbing?"

"My apartment is in the basement."

"Jesus fucking Christ." The man wiped his face with the palm of his hand. "I was so happy five minutes ago. What the hell happened."

"Look," Hillary said in a soothing tone of voice. "I'm sorry for eating your lunch. Lunches. But to be fair, I didn't know there were two of you."

"Yeah, and while we're on the subject, what's up with that?" I asked. "Are you guys twins or something? Because if so, you don't seem very remorseful about his, uh, passing. Not that I'm judging you."

"You might call us twins, though that hardly begins to explain it. Actually…"

"You guys, I'm sorry to interrupt," Hillary interrupted, "but I'm about to have a situation here."

"Alright, here we go." The man said. "We're all going downstairs, you two first. And at the risk of boring my audience with repetition, let me remind you I have no problem shooting women in the back."

"How progressive of you."

Approaching the sofa, Hillary reached for the picture frame that activated the trap door.

"Hold on a second," the man barked. "What're you

doing? Going for a wall safe? Maybe have something in there that'll put some holes in me?"

"The entrance to the basement is hidden, this picture opens it."

"*Where* does it open?"

She didn't answer. He pushed back the hammer on my gun and put its barrel against my head.

"Right there." She sighed, looking at the ground beneath his feet."

"And I would've fallen through the hole I guess?"

Hillary shrugged.

"Nice try," he said, walking closer to the wall so he could see what she was doing. "But you'd have to get up pretty early in the morning…"

Hillary pushed the frame and the same hole I'd fallen through opened up and the man fell through it.

"Come on!" She grabbed my arm and we ran out of the cabin. The van was there and the keys were in it. "It won't take him long to get out of there, but it'll take hours to find a way out of these woods without a vehicle."

The van was late model and it started immediately, so we managed to dodge at least the one cliché. Instead of taking the well-worn dirt road, Hillary turned the van off into the woods. Seemed like a weird choice, but I trusted her.

"You were saying?" Hillary said after several minutes of silence.

"I didn't say anything."

"No, that's what I should've said to him when he fell in the hole. If I'd thought of it in time."

"You want to go back?"

"Nah." Hillary sighed, squinting into the sun. "*L'esprit d'escalier.*"

Once again I didn't know what she was talking about, and I had the feeling that would often be the case with her. But there was another feeling as well, and it then it hit me.

"Actually, we have to go back." I said.

"Seriously, I'm over it."

"No, it's something else. Something important."

"Sarah, I'm sorry for eating all your Tums, but we can get more, I promise you."

"I'm sure I'll eventually forgive you for that, but there were some documents Melania gave me."

"They weren't by any chance covered in dick drawings and ketchup stains?"

"How'd you know that?"

Reaching into her jacket, which still looked amazing despite everything, she pulled out the aforementioned papers.

"Amazing! Of course, it would've been nice to hold onto the diary too, but I guess it's not worth risking our lives for."

She reached back into her jacket and triumphantly showed me the diary.

"How'd the hell did you manage that?"

"When will you learn to stop underestimating me?"

"Now," I said. "Just now."

Love Underground

In a subterranean computer lab well beneath the deepest recesses of the White House there were people reading and writing emails. The content of the emails differed, but the collective goal was singular: acquiring intel regarding the parallel universe and its apparent attempt to combine/manipulate this one. While the mission was of the highest possible importance, the actual work being done was of a somewhat ignoble nature. Mostly consisting of romantic correspondence with specific targets and the extraction of actionable information. Which wouldn't be meaningfully different than standard espionage except for the fact that the general population had no idea their very reality was in danger, and for the time being it was deemed important that things remain that way.

Dressed in identical genderless jumpsuits, the agents clicked away, a chaotic symphony of keyboards that could make you feel crazy if you started thinking about it. The absence of human voices was conspicuous.

"I might have something." A single voice pierced through the raga-like hum.

A tall, tired looking man in a rumpled suit minimized the game of FreeCell he'd been playing and reluctantly pushed himself out of his chair. If this was another false alert he'd have the kid fired. And considering they'd been at it for months with nothing to show, chances were very good the kid was done for.

"I might have something, Sir." The agent said as his supervisor approached.

"Yeah, Roger, I heard you the first time. I heard you fart half an hour ago. This is a small office. Speaking of which," the man clapped his hands to get everyone's attention. "People, I don't know if it's a question of diet or the need for medical attention, but can we please try to tone down the flatulence? It's starting to affect my sleep, honestly."

Nobody wanted to acknowledge it was them being addressed, so nobody answered. The tall man sighed.

"Anyway, what was it you wanted to show me? Another unemployed racist whose neighbor's been acting *ethnic?*"

"No, Sir. Actually, I've been working on a target I suspected of having security clearance. A particle physicist. Turns out he's actually with CERN."

"Are you serious?" The tall man gasped. "Don't tell me…"

"Sir, he worked on the Hadron Collider. As far back

as oh-eight. Sir, not only does he openly reveal that he knows about the paradox, he specifically mentions it. And well, I think you should just read what I've got here."

Email from Dr. Frank Dunbar:

"It had been four years since we activated the Large Hadron Collider and the glamour had significantly faded. Time was I could walk into any bar in the Geneva area, flap my lab coat around a little (we weren't really supposed to wear them out and about, but a man has needs) and wind up going home for brief, perfunctory sex with any number of the hygienic and frosty Swiss babes who were so ubiquitous back then. We were on the cutting edge and we all knew it. All felt the same insane electricity flowing through us, colliding particles at a rate never before known. To say that things have devolved somewhat since then would be an understatement. I recently caught an intern trying to collide a ham sandwich with a dildo, to give you an idea of where we're at these days. And he didn't even seem to be enjoying himself. He wasn't the only one monkeying around, to be fair. Pretty much everyone was taking their turns, colliding whatever two objects interested them at the moment. Dr. Whitney tried her best to keep us in line, but someone had snagged a vial of LSD from an innovative management seminar and so what started out as experiments in microdosing soon became

a pretty solid routine of regular dosing. Just try to wrangle a hundred scientists who are tripping balls and colliding sandwiches, see how far you get. Eventually she gave up and soon she was worse than any of us. She wanted to invent a new form of birth control that was also an amphetamine. And for a while we were convinced that she'd succeeded, but then she found out that she was just infertile, and that she'd been boning the locals for no reason (except to pass the time while suffering from what turned out to be pretty serious come-downs). I guess what I'm trying to say, is that nobody should've really been that shocked when we accidentally caused a schism in the space/time continuum. And frankly, I'm not sorry. The parallel reality we tapped into is my favorite thing to watch, though I am grateful I don't have to live there. In order to differentiate we've taken to replacing the '1' in the year with an exclamation point (20!2, 20!8, etc...) which though grammatically confusing, really nails the tone. If we haven't repaired the rift in the next couple years we'll have to think of something else, but it's difficult to think that far ahead with this intense birth control serum coursing through my veins. And honestly, there's a good chance none of us will be around long enough for any of that to be necessary. It's come to our attention that a second Large Collider (possibly even bigger) has been constructed deep underground in the vicinity of the White House, in the U.S. As far as we can tell, this duality of colliders could either repair the rift, or completely obliterate both worlds, and potentially countless others. So far, we've been unable to actually communicate with anyone on the other side to share intelligence, but based on what we've seen, we aren't hopeful they have any. For example, in our reality Donald J. Trump is a disgraced former professional wrestler, once known as The Orange Bastard, now a commentator on one of the lesser cable networks. And he can just barely manage that. In 20!8 he's the fucking president of the United States of America. I mean, try to wrap your mind around that. Whenever I turn on the monitors and see him, I laugh so hard that I get a hernia. I'm serious, that actually happened. A hernia! But I also acknowledge that it's only funny from such a vast and theoretical distance. I can't imagine what the people living in 20!8 must be going through. I mean, Berenstain Bears? What sense does that make? I'd like to do anything I can to help them, but our first priority must be making sure none of Trump's supporters make it through into our reality. If it were possible to rescue a certain number of the others, that might be something, but then you get into all kinds of ethical issues and it's a total headache. Well, that's all for now!"

"So, he knows about the paradox but doesn't realize

you're on the other side? Which he's calling 20!8? How the hell do you pronounce that, anyway?"

"I don't know. And no, he doesn't realize. I'm pretty sure he also thinks I'm a woman."

"Why would he think that?"

"He said something about seeing a fancy bra he thinks I'd look good in. Also, I'm calling myself Taylor Swift."

"Like *the* Taylor Swift?"

"Yeah. Well, she's not famous on his side, I guess."

"Still."

"I know."

"You mean to say this poor bastard not only can't meet a girl in real life, he can't even get catfished in his own reality?"

"Yeah. It's pretty sad if you think too much about it, so I try not to."

"Understandable. So, what actionable intel have you gotten?"

"Well, none."

"So what value does this project have?"

"I mean, nothing you would really call *value*, per se. It's fun?"

"Right. The thing is, performance reviews are coming up, and if we're going to continue to get funding we need something tangible to show. You know the president isn't interested in ideas."

"He says he's coming to Nashville for a conference, and he wants to meet me in person."

"The president?"

"No, Doctor Dunbar."

"He wants to meet Taylor Swift, you mean?"

"Yeah."

"I can understand that. Is there any chance you could get him to go to DC?"

"Probably."

"Interesting. Okay, I'll get back to you on that. In the meantime, keep this to yourself. And in the off chance that you run into the president, don't mention anything about any Berenstain bears. Nothing about bears at all. And for godsake don't call him Goldilocks."

"Copy that. Oh, one more thing, Sir. When you say keep this to myself, do you mean I can't tell anyone?"

"Yes, Roger, that is what the phrase means."

"The thing is, I might've already told a couple people. It was just so funny…"

"Who have you told?"

"Well, pretty much everyone down here has printouts of the emails, and my brother in law saw one I'd left on the kitchen table. He just thinks it's a weird novel I'm working on, though."

"God help you if this thing gets away from us. And if it turns out that your brother in law has to be neutralized, I'm going to be looking at you. And you might as well print me out a copy, if everyone has one anyway."

"Yes, Sir."

A Man at a Loss

Limping through the woods, the man repeatedly checked his phone for a signal. Using GPS to find a way out would be good, but more importantly he wanted to check his email. Despite the inconveniences he'd recently encountered, the man felt more confident than ever that his plan would come to fruition. Nothing that had happened so far could possibly compromise that. However, the biggest, most grotesque, obstacle loomed ahead of him. Donald. Goldilocks. By all appearances the man seemed hardly capable of dressing himself, let alone thwarting an elegant and perfect plan whose careful architecture had been drawn over the course of several ascetic years. And yet, there he was, occupying the White House.

They'd struck up a pen pal situation almost a year ago, and the president's responses were either maddeningly laconic, or so effusively reminiscent of a childlike worldview that at times the man had to wonder if he'd accidentally been corresponding with Kanye West. The man had taken the time and patience to finally broach the topic of the collider, not to mention the time he'd taken to establish himself as a tech magnate, his image gracing the cover of more than one under-read industry journal. By now he should've been made a consultant at least, possibly even a member of the inner cabinet, filling the void left by Musk when he decided he'd rather play with pop-stars and flame-throwers than influence policy.

But the president hadn't taken the bait. He seemed happier gossiping about movie stars and complaining about his digestion than changing the future of the human fucking narrative. He was clearly a master tactician, with unbelievable levels of patience and reserve. To so consistently play the role of illiterate and irritable idiot could only be accomplished by a true Machiavellian genius, on a level with Iago. It was Shakespearean. To gain the trust of such a man, with the explicit purpose of betraying him, would require all the skills and cunning the man had. And even then, it would be the most difficult undertaking of his life. But it was necessary. He already had a contact within the subterranean intelligence network, but to actually gain physical access—without which he couldn't possibly succeed—would require help from the most powerful man in the world.

His goal was so close now, he could practically smell the heady tang of illicit sex wafting off the presidential desk. But he knew that this was the time when people tend to make the gravest errors. He had to remind himself to take a breath, move cautiously. Patting his pocket to reassure himself he still had a backup of the tape, the man exhaled in relief. Losing the other copy had been sloppy of him. Not to mention the van. But it didn't matter. If things came down to blackmail, he had ammunition of the highest order.

But first he had to find a way out of these godforsaken woods. Then he would take his plan to the next step: conning perhaps the wiliest conman the world had ever known. A devilish player who at this very moment was almost certainly effecting machinations that would make the man's path more treacherous than ever.

Bear Stains

Donald had just received some very disturbing news. It involved something called the Mandela Effect, and not only did its pernicious influence corrupt his favorite movies, Forest Gump and Field of Dreams (the phrase "if you build it they will cum" had been the NorthStar of his entire life), but it also had something to do with bears. As far as Donald was concerned, bears were the most evil creatures to ever exist, right after his own family members. And this Mandela thingy didn't just involve regular bears, they were stained bears. Bear stains. He didn't know what the hell that meant, and he didn't want to know. He just wanted it to stop. His best bet was to consult the smartest person he knew.

"Son," he said, entering Barron's room, despite such invasions being expressly verboten. "I need to discuss something serious with you. What do you know about bears?"

"Bears?" The child asked, surreptitiously hiding a stack of books and several envelopes he was apparently filling with flour. "Ursus, in the family Ursidae? An omnivorous mammal of the Chordata phylum? Not much really, why?"

"Oh, nothing. I didn't think you'd be able to help. Thanks anyway."

"Dad?" Barron asked. "Are you okay?"

"I don't know, Son." He answered honestly. "I don't know."

Vanilla Ice

Hillary didn't say anything for a long time after we'd read the email/audio transcript. I assumed she was either thinking about it, was shaken from the day's events, or was still suffering from the extra portion of enchiladas. Possibly a perfect storm of everything mentioned.

"There was something about that guy." Hillary said absently, as if talking to herself. "Guys, I mean."

"What's the problem, haven't you ever banged…I mean, seen twins before?"

"They weren't twins." She said. "They were the same person."

"I don't understand. What does that mean?"

"It means they've figured out how to pass between realities. It means that things are happening faster than we thought."

Somehow people on the other side had figured out how to cross over. And the only person we knew who could do it, we'd left in a heap in the cabin. Which in retrospect was maybe a bit hasty. So hasty, in fact, that I had a hard time believing HR could be responsible for such a blunder.

"Forgive me for saying so, but I get the feeling there's still something you're not telling me."

Hillary snorted.

"There are a lot of things I'm not telling you. Deciding what things to tell which people is pretty much the majority of my job."

"Well, I guess when you put it that way it sounds reasonable. But it's still frustrating. I've given up a lot for The Order, and frankly I don't enjoy feeling like I'm still playing second string."

"That's totally understandable." Hillary agreed. I waited for her to continue, but she didn't.

"Fine, if that's how we're going to be." I said, popping a tape out of the van's tape deck and replacing it with my personal mix.

"Who the hell plays tapes anymore?" Hillary snapped moodily.

"Well, me, obviously." I said. "And apparently our new friend."

We drove for a few minutes, listening to Fleetwood Mac. Blessed, speechless minutes. Suddenly Hillary smacked the stereo, popping my tape out.

"Whoa!" I gasped. "What the hell are you doing?"

"There is no good reason there would be a tape deck in such a new van." She said, her blue-gray eyes piercing the horizon. I sensed a vast and frenetic machinery moving behind those eyes.

"Some people still like them." I protested, starting to take her attack a little personally. "What's it to you, anyway?"

"Was there already a tape in there?"

"Yeah," I said, fishing around on the floorboard for the Vanilla Ice tape the guy had apparently been listening to.

"Put the tape in."

"You can't be serious?" I frowned. "I'm as ironic as the next Alaskan snowmobile aficionado, but *Vanilla Ice?*"

"Just do it." Hillary sighed.

"Fine."

I put the tape in but nothing happened. The only sound was a dull metallic hiss from the tape itself, and some barely audible scratching sounds.

"What's the deal?"

"Cassette tapes were used by spies toward the end of the cold war. Embedded information that can't be read by a regular tape player."

"Yeah, I mean, I knew that," I lied.

Hillary popped the tape out and slipped it into her jacket pocket.

"You know anybody who can read that thing for us?"

"I do." She said. "But you're not coming with me. I've got another job for you."

"Can I stop pretending to be an illiterate Republican?" I asked hopefully.

"Let's not get ahead of ourselves." She shook her head. "I need you to go back to Washington and find out as much as you can about the email transcript you showed me. If people are crossing over, we need to know how. Getting to the bottom of that transcript is our best bet. The operatives involved with the program are apparently unaware that they're being recorded, which means the order must come from the top. As you can imagine I'm in no position to visit the White House, so you'll have to expand your contact with the First Lady. Also, I wasn't lying earlier, we're going to need to find a hygienic place to pull over."

"There's a Denny' up ahead." I told her. "Does that work for you?"

"Goddamnit…"

Mall Crue

This time when I returned to the White House it was through the front gates. We'd decided it would be safer and easier if my cover included being friends with Melania. Besides, Goldilocks had been having graphic nightmares about bears coming through the walls, and it wasn't too difficult to imagine what the cause of that might've been.

Security finally waved me through and directed me to guest check-in, where the First Lady met me and took me to the residence. Being officially allowed was better in certain regards, but it also meant not having access to the oval office. As we walked in, the vice president was leaving the bathroom, wiping his mouth on a napkin, which he then tossed in a wastebasket. Apparently, he refused to use his own bathroom when women guests were around, and when he saw Melania and me he made a wide circle around us, his eyes downcast, refusing to acknowledging our existence.

Which was fine with me.

If anything could've possibly given me an even lower opinion of the man, the fact that he apparently ate food in the bathroom was just the thing to do it. Out of curiosity I peeked at the branded napkin he'd left. It was from Pizza X, the notoriously bad place next door to the Victoria's Secret.

The one with the hidden entrance that no one outside of The Order was supposed to know about? How would Mike Pence have discovered a secret passage in a woman's lingerie store?

"Actually," Melania said, glancing around the gaudily furnished residence, which looked more like a Dubai brothel than the home of a sitting president. "I hate it here. Want to go somewhere?"

"Is that safe?"

"Safer out there than in here, at least." She shrugged.

"I'm not so sure about that." I said. "I just saw a headline about some guy stalking Taylor Swift. Claimed he worked on the Hadron Collider and that they had been exchanging emails for months. Seems like scientists are collecting pop stars these days."

"Who else?" She asked innocently. I started to wonder if she'd even read the documents she'd given me.

"Elon Musk, for one. And, well, just him I guess."

"Can he really even being called a scientist?" She asked. "Seems more like engineer with aggrandized sense of self-importance."

"Those last five words characterize pretty much every dude I've ever met, so…"

"True," She acknowledged. "But he's like, a special case."

"Fair enough. You want to go get a smoothie?" I asked.

"Walk around the mall?"

"Eh…"

"There's a sale at Sephora."

"Alright, fine." She said. "I need to exchange a swimsuit anyway."

"Can you exchange swimsuits?"

"You can if you don't tell anyone you're already wearing it."

"Oh…okay?" I said. I'd given up trying to understand her.

Despite the potential compromise to my cover identity I ordered some wheat grass at the Jamba Juice. I realized I hadn't eaten any vegetables in several weeks, and my poor diet was beginning to take a toll. Besides, I could always blame it on Melania, if there were any photos. As we waited I noticed an attractive young man standing nearby. It wasn't the fact that he noticed us that caught my eye, or his too perfect beard and man-bun. After all, I was with the First Lady of the United States, and we were flanked by Secret Service agents. It would've been strange if people didn't notice us. What was unusual about the man was exactly how disinterested he seemed to be. Perhaps he could simply have been showing respect by minding his own business, but that idea sounded completely bogus the moment I thought it.

Despite what she'd said, the cashier at Pac Sun was

disinclined to refund Melania on a bathing suit she was already wearing, and the manager didn't disagree no matter how heated Melania got. And she got plenty heated. At first I tried to calm her down, which of course had the opposite effect. Then I noticed the same young man in workwear that I'd seen next to the Jamba Juice. It was possible that he was just a regular gaper, but for some reason I didn't think so. My instincts told me his interests were more than carnal. I could've simply alerted secret service and had them detain him, but that would've made it impossible to learn anything from him. I watched the man close the distance between us, but never getting too close. But he also didn't seem to care if we noticed him. I needed to get him away from both the crowd and the secret service. Finally, my patience wore thin and I made my move.

"I'm so sorry about this," I whispered to the cashier.

Taking a deep breath, because I'm honestly not a horrible person, I swept my arm across the counter, clearing it of all the small products on the counter. Everything went crashing to the floor with more commotion than I'd anticipated. Some of those little lipsticks can really bounce.

"Do you have any idea who you're dealing with?" I shouted at the poor cashier, in whose eyes I could sense the suffering of betrayal. I could already imagine what the headlines would be, but for better or worse we were way beyond negative headlines.

Almost immediately the secret service agents were ushering us out of the store. I noticed a hallway with a restroom sign.

"We need to use the ladies' room." I told the agents, who looked to Melania for confirmation. "What, is my word that I need to use the bathroom not good enough for you? Good grief, man, I was almost your boss."

"Operative word, *almost*." One of the agents said, a smirk playing across his rather sinuous lips.

"Christ," I said. "You get paid extra for the wit?"

He shook his head.

"Nevertheless, there's a bathroom right there, and that's where we're going. And you're not coming with us." I was trying to keep an eye on the interloper as I berated yet another person who didn't deserve it, but at some point he'd slipped away. But now I realized I actually needed to use the bathroom.

"What's your deal?" Melania asked once the door had closed behind us.

"Sorry about that," I said. "I needed to get rid of them for a minute. I saw someone watching us."

"Oh." She said, looking at the ground. She didn't seem surprised. "Was he about this tall, and dressed like out of work lumberjack with trust fund?"

"Yes." I said. "That's exactly what he looked like."

"Out of work lumberjack?" The man shouted in incredulous English tinged with some kind of eastern bloc accent, dramatically kicking out the door on a stall where he'd apparently been hiding. Or rather, he tried to dramatically kick out the door, not realizing that it opened inward rather than out. I reached for my pistol, which of course I didn't have. Melania was still surprisingly unperturbed.

"Who the hell is this?" I demanded.

She didn't answer me. Instead she shouted something in Russian to the man, who seemed pretty chastened. He said something back to her, also in Russian, and left the bathroom in a huff, his man-bun whipping around.

"He's actually good agent," Melania shrugged. "Most of time."

"Tell me what's going on."

Melania confessed that she'd recently been activated by her Russian handlers. To what end she didn't say, though it didn't require the greatest imagination, considering her marital status.

"To be honest," she sighed. "Had forgotten about them. Had hoped they'd forgotten too. Was my mistake. Should've realized that Russians never forget anything."

"Didn't you just tell me that *you* forgot?"

"Am not Russian, am Bulgarian. Bulgarians forget

everything."

"I doubt we have time before those guys get curious about what's taking us so long, but you have a lot to explain."

Melania nodded. There was something about her that I didn't trust, whether because of or in spite of her confession, it didn't matter. I felt conflicted about doing it, but on our way out of the bathroom I planted a bug on the back of her neck. It was very small and almost impossible to find. I wouldn't be able to see anything, but I'd be able to hear everything.

At Your Cervix

Things were too hot to meet at the DC headquarters, so I was instructed to head north to a small town outside of Philadelphia, where The Order maintained an annex in the basement of a medical building. There were five separate offices in the building, each with its own specialty.

"Can I help you?" An annoyed looking office manager asked, glaring at me between sliding panes of frosted glass. I hadn't been told which office to ask for.

"Uh," I quickly scanned the list of clinics. Probably it wasn't the urologist, at least. Then at the bottom of the sign I saw a listing for an obstetrician, dubiously titled At Your Cervix. I took a deep breath and rolled the dice. "Um, I'm looking for At Your Cervix?"

"Oh." The woman said, her tone and facial expression softening. "First floor, right down this hall to your left."

"Thank you." I said.

"No, *thank you*." She replied, holding eye contact. "Seriously, thank you."

We exchanged a knowing smile.

There was another woman sitting behind a desk in the waiting room, which looked like the waiting room of any medical office.

"Do you have an appointment?" She asked.

"Yes," I said. "I think so. Sarah P..."

"Of course." She said. "Could you please press your thumb against this pad."

"It's not going to poke me or anything is it?"

"No."

"Okay," I hesitated, shakily extending my thumb towards what looked like a watch face embedded in the counter. When I touched the surface of the pad a tiny needle immediately popped out and poked my thumb. "Goddamnit," I said, sucking my wounded thumb. "What the hell? I could've swore you just told me I wouldn't get poked."

"I told you what you wanted to hear," she shrugged, typing something on her keyboard. "You knew in your heart you were gonna get poked."

"That's...doesn't...nevermind."

She flashed me a thin smile and buzzed open a door.

"Down the hall, third door on the left."

Behind the door was a cement staircase descending in darkness, which is just a goddamn lawsuit waiting to happen if you ask me. As I carefully made my way down the steps a dim light appeared above me and I managed to reach the bottom without breaking my neck. What I found was a fully functional intelligence gathering operation, with half a dozen women. In the center of the room there was a large round table, where Hillary was conferring with a skinny balding guy who might've been thirteen or thirty. He looked vaguely like Buffalo Bill from The Silence of the Lambs.

"News?" Hillary asked without looking up. She was wearing a fresh pantsuit that was somehow even more flattering than her previous one.

"I didn't get much of anything out of her," I said, looking for something in my pocket that I already knew wasn't there. "But I did manage to plant a bug on her neck."

"A bug?" Hillary asked, looking at me for the first time. "Bugging a fellow sister is highly unusual. And on her neck?"

"She has a lot of neck, it was a prime target."

"Did you have a good reason for bugging her?"

"Well, it turns out that she's been a Russian sleeper agent the whole time, and she was recently activated. Does that seem like a good reason?"

"Yes." Hillary sighed, turning to her unfortunate looking technical assistant. "Activate any bugs that have been deployed in the last forty-eight hours."

Apparently the volume had been left all the way up because the room was immediately flooded with the cacophony of what sounded like a tropical rainstorm. I could hear Melania's voice, but I couldn't tell if she was drowning or singing.

"What is that?" The tech asked. "Is she hurt?"

"I think she's in the shower." Hillary said.

"Thunderballs and lightnings really super frightening for me Galileo GALILEO!"

"Is she trying to sing Bohemian Rhapsody?"

"For legal reasons, no she isn't. Don't mention it again."

"Fine, sorry."

"Okay, we'll come back to that." Hillary said, muting the audio. "Let me know if anything interesting happens. In the meantime, take a look at what we got from that Vanilla Ice tape."

She pulled up a screen and played a video file. The footage was of a middle-aged man wearing a lab coat with no shirt on under it, coincidentally listening to Vanilla Ice. He was either having a seizure or practicing his pop-and-lock routine. Or possibly both.

"There's more data on here," the IT said. "But unfortunately it's been corrupted."

"Hacker?" I asked.

IT shook his head. "Looks like something's been spilled on it. If I had to guess I'd say Mountain Dew."

"No shit?" I mumbled in what I hoped was an innocent

tone of voice, praying nobody would remember my many public speeches extolling the fluorescent green beverage.

"Nevermind that. Look here," Hillary said, pausing the video and pointing at the upper left section of the screen. On the wall was a plaque with the official insignia of CERN.

"The Hadron Collider." I said.

Hillary nodded.

"We think this is the same scientist from the emails, and that he's figured out a way to cross the parallel."

"Holy shit," I said, the gravity of the discovery settling on me. "This is it, right? Is this it?"

"This might be it." She said. "And we wouldn't have this if you hadn't insisted on listening to your mixtape. So, thank you for that."

"Yeah, well. No big deal."

"Modesty doesn't really suit you, does it?"

"I've been told that before, yes."

"So," Hillary said to her IT. "Anything interesting?"

"Well," he said. "I think she might've masturbated. It was kind of interesting."

"And you listened to her?" Hillary frowned.

"I mean, you told me to listen. I don't know, what should I..."

"I have to say, I'm a little shocked at you. I thought you

were better than that."

Hillary winked at me while the poor guy stammered incomprehensibly.

"Unbelievable." I said, shaking my head.

"I'm sorry." He said, looking at his hands.

"Hold on," Hillary said. "What's that? Turn it up."

The sound was staticky, but we could hear what were definitely human voices. Vaguely Russian sounding.

"You're overthinking this." A man's voice said.

"No one's ever telling me this before." A woman's voice, her accent thick and difficult to believe. Unmistakably belonging to Melania.

"And another thing," the man went on. "Why do you talk like that? It's ridiculous. We spent a fortune training you to talk like them, and you're even worse than before! Not even my deranged grandfather speaks like this!"

The audio went staticky and we couldn't hear anything.

"They were talking for a minute before, but there must be something wrong with the bug."

"Fuck! What is up with these things?"

"They're made in America."

"Oh."

"There's one other thing. Did you plant any other bugs recently?"

"No." Hillary said, looking at me.

"Nope," I said. "Only the one."

"Why do you ask?"

"You told me to activate all the bugs deployed in the last forty-eight hours, and this wasn't the only one."

"Well can you get audio?"

He shook his head.

"This one's even worse than the other. Nothing but static. However, the bugs also have GPS signals, and this one's on the move." He pulled up a real-time map showing the bug, which seemed to not be moving at all. "It *was* moving, I swear. Seems to have stopped now. Somewhere in Manhattan. Actually, as far as I can tell it's directly under the East River. But that doesn't make sense."

"Actually, it does." Hillary said, looking at her watch. "If we leave now we can get there in an hour."

"An hour?" I coughed. "That's impossible."

"It's not if I'm driving. Dennis, go pull my car around."

"Do you need me to come with you?" He asked, starting to pack his bag.

"No." She shook her head. "Just go, like, get everyone some sandwiches or something."

"Oh, ok." He said, his shoulders slumping.

"Dennis, am I sensing attitude?"

"No, ma'am."

"*Ma'am?*"

"I mean sir…I mean…"

"Just go get the goddamn car."

She waited until he'd gone and then she quietly told me, "Where we're going is only for the very select few. Which means it's time for you to join the fully initiated."

"What're you talking about?"

"I'm talking about the inner circle. I'm talking about the Sisters of Athena."

The Inner Circle

I guess I shouldn't have been surprised to discover that Hillary can drive. Like, *really* drive. I don't think she dropped below a hundred miles an hour until we approached The Holland Tunnel.

"We'll be stuck forever if you take the tunnel." I warned her.

"Still a doubting Debbie." She sighed, pressing a button on her console. A section of the tunnel's wall opened and she steered into it. I watched the passage close behind us.

"What the hell else have I been missing out on?" I asked, a bit wounded.

"A lot. But don't start crying on me, I need you alert."

The auxiliary tunnel guided us deep under Manhattan, I was told. I had to take her word for it because there weren't any windows. Finally we reached some kind of underground parking lot. There was a lone car parked there. An Audi of indeterminate vintage. I'm not officially allowed to know anything about European imports.

When we got out I put my hand on the hood of the car. It was cold, but that didn't necessarily mean anything because the parking lot was freezing. I looked inside, but it had been cleared out. Even the glove compartment and sunglasses storage thing were empty. There was a key left in the ignition.

"Who knows," I said. "This might've been down here for years."

Hillary shook her head.

"It's a two-thousand-sixteen model. And this facility was decommissioned eight years ago."

Approaching what looked like an elevator, Hillary pressed her thumb against a button and winced when it poked her. As the door opened she reached into her jacket and pulled out a familiar looking pistol.

"Hey," I said. "Is that mine?"

She looked at it.

"Oh, uh, yeah." She looked at the weapon, pretending to be surprised by it. "It's a sweet little piece."

"I know," I said. "I had it custom made."

"God, is this going to be the Tums episode all over again? Why are you so obsessed with possessions?"

"You never had siblings, did you?"

"Two little brothers."

"Fine, you hold onto it."

We stepped into the elevator, but when the doors shut it didn't feel like we were going up or down, but rather sideways. After a long minute the doors opened up and released us into a frankly massive surveillance center. Banks of monitors lined one wall, with a large control panel in the middle. Everything was lit up and the sound of computers whirring was nearly deafening.

"Doesn't look very decommissioned." I noted.

"I don't *feel* very decommissioned." A robotic voice issued from somewhere.

"This isn't possible." Hillary said quietly, checking the room for anyone who might be hiding. There was nobody there.

"What is this place, anyway?"

"Yeah, just go ahead and talk about me like I'm not sitting right here." The robot voice said in a defiant tone.

"You're looking at the most comprehensive surveillance system ever created. From here we can access any live camera in the world, activate any webcam. Even closed circuit stuff. The system was developed for reasons of security, but to be honest, some sisters might've used it for somewhat more personal reasons."

"Like what?"

"Like catching significant others *in flagrante*, for one."

"No shit…"

"We ultimately decided that the invasion of privacy was too great and the whole thing was taken offline."

"You can really spy on anyone?"

"Pretty much." She said. "Why, you want to see what your husband's up to?"

I thought about it.

"No." I said. "No, I don't."

"Afraid of what you'll see?"

"I'm starting to realize that I might actually care about him." I admitted. "And to be honest, I haven't exactly been an angel myself. If we make it through this, I'm going to have a whole different kind of situation to deal with, and I don't want it to be based on spying."

"Admirable."

"Who had the ability to bring it back online, anyway?"

"Nobody." She said. "Nobody but me."

"Is it possible that it *was* you? The other you?"

"I…don't know. But I can check. System, who brought you back online?"

"Well I'm just fine," the system's voice said in a

sarcastic tone. "Thank you so much for asking."

"I'm not sure what the bigger mistake was, creating the system in the first place, or giving it a male voice."

"I could talk like this if you like?" The system said in the lilt of a young Irish girl. "Or maybe like this." Now it was a wise sounding Jamaican woman.

"Either of those would be great, actually."

"I was joking!" It whined in its male voice. "Gosh!"

"Forget the voice!" Hillary snapped. "Just tell me who brought you back online."

"Fine," the system moped. "I was brought online twenty minutes ago, and the authorization is logged as: Dr. Kelly Whitney."

"Weird." I said. "I went to high school with a Kelly Whitney. She's definitely not a doctor though."

"What kind of person is she?"

"She gives out raisins on Halloween."

Hillary grimaced.

"At least it wasn't you." I said. "The other you, I mean."

"Cold comfort." Hillary said. "I know the names of every member of The Order, and there's no Kelly Whitney. There's Kelly Ripa, and Kelly Kapowski—a codename—but no Kelly Whitney."

"I don't know what to say." The system said. "I only do what I'm told."

"Fine. Show me all the cameras that have been accessed since you've been back online."

"Only two cameras have been accessed."

"Well bring them up then."

An image appeared on a large screen. I immediately recognized my own living room. It was empty of life except for the dog, who was joyfully licking himself on my oriental rug. Then Todd appeared, wearing a tank-top and cowboy hat, but naked from the waist down. He was eating a corndog, drinking a beer, and singing a once popular country song about having friends in low places. Any one of these activities on its own would've seemed ignoble, but put all together I found myself at least mildly impressed. However, this stuff wasn't meant for public consumption.

"Go ahead and switch to the next camera, please!"

The screen flashed and I couldn't tell at first what I was looking at. If I had to wager I would've guessed it was an Oompa Loompa with a glandular disorder and a clinical sweat problem. It seemed to be rifling through a chest of drawers, probably in search of hard drugs. Because, come on, have you seen those fucking guys?

"It's the White House." Hillary said.

"Are you sure?" I asked, squinting at the screen.

"I lived there for eight years, remember."

"Holy shit." I realized what I was looking at. It was him. Trump. And he, too, was naked (what the hell is up with dudes, anyway?) His entire body was as orange as a desert sunset, but greasier. He was like a jack-o-lantern covered in baby oil.

"Try not to throw up on the instruments if you can help it." Hillary said, making a recording of the horror show. I didn't know why, and I didn't want to know.

I looked around for a trashcan while Hillary checked her messages. She wasn't pleased.

"I can't find her."

"Find who?" I asked, struggling against the taste of bile rising in my throat.

"Who do you think? Taylor Swift. If the alt version of that scientist has a thing for her, we can only assume this one does as well. That could be very useful when it comes to convincing him to help us. Or at least it would have. Fortunately, I have a backup plan." She said, looking me up and down.

"Just so you know, I'm not very popular in Europe."

"Is there anywhere that you *are* popular? No offense."

"Let me remind you I was crowned Miss Wasilla. And that was long before I ever even heard of The Order."

"Of course." Hillary rolled her eyes. "Who could forget."

"I also do okay in rural Alabama. Parts of Ohio. Arizona." Saying the state's name reminded me of the last time I'd been there. The day everything went sideways.

"By the way, I've been meaning to say, I'm sorry about Maverick." Hillary said. "I know you guys were close. By the time this is done, we'll get the motherfucker that killed him. With any luck it'll be the same person we're already after."

"Thank you for saying that. I haven't really even had time to think about it, what with the parallel universe and everything."

"Right, right." Hillary nodded. "By the way, did you guys ever...?"

"No," I snapped. "Of course not. Don't be ridiculous. I mean, you're making me laugh out loud here. Seriously, holy shit."

"Whoa," Hillary showed me her palms. "A simple no would've sufficed. Methinks the lady doth, well, you know. Anyway, your popularity—or lack thereof—is inconsequential. Thanks to your episode at the mall you've had an unexpected resurgence in fame. In order to travel under the radar, you're going to need a bit of a makeover."

"Oh, okay. Actually, that sounds kind of nice. It's been a while since I've been able to change up my look."

"You might want to wait to see what I have in mind before you get too excited."

On our way out, Hillary uploaded what would soon be infamously known as "the Goldilocks video". She's always two steps ahead.

The Second Cabin

The moment he made it within cell tower distance the man's phone started vibrating uncontrollably with news that the president had tweeted a video of himself. At first he thought that It was his blackmail video, and that his once formidable ammunition would be rendered impotent. But it turned out to be far worse than that.

The man had a horrible, helpless feeling. Like he could do pullups until his arms exploded and it wouldn't change anything. Wouldn't change him, wouldn't change his life. Wouldn't change the fact that he was either being played by a master manipulator the likes of which he'd never encountered (and he'd lived in Silicon Valley for several years), or he'd egregiously overestimated perhaps the single most diseased and dysfunctional intellect in the known species, and effectively played himself.

The first option provided somewhat more comfort, but he couldn't help but think that he'd been living in dream and this was just more wishful thinking. How the hell could this have happened? Trump was like Mr. Magoo with severe body dysmorphia and a taste for human blood. The fact that he had anticipated the man's plan to blackmail him, and preempted him with a far worse video, was a tactical twist the man had not anticipated. And the fact that the president was now using the footage—some kind of greasy burlesque that could scandalize the most prurient of the Berlin party sect—as proof of his own virility, was something else altogether.

The man had an irresistible urge to do something outrageous and bizarre. Something self-destructive. Something with severe consequences. Defenestration. The word popped into his head. To throw oneself through a window. He looked around. No windows, which had been the whole point of using this cabin. Aside from one tiny thing about six feet up, the logistics of throwing himself out of which were unthinkable, even to an engineer of his abilities. Defenestration would have to wait until later, assuming he still felt the same way.

"You seem upset," a girl's voice said. "You want to talk about it?"

"Jesus Christ!" The man gasped, clutching his chest. With everything going on he'd completely forgotten about his hostage. Which in itself was amazing, because she'd turned out to be the most annoying hostage he'd ever encountered.

"I could write you a song about it." She offered.

"No! No more fucking songs. I told you about that."

"Too late." She said, starting to sing. "He was a mean man/with a stupid plan/can't do anything right/just does what he can…"

Queer Eyes

We pulled into an underground parking garage in midtown and took an elevator to the penthouse. The loft we stepped into was chic and modern, as were the three men waiting for us. They were crowded around a laptop with their hands over their mouths. Even so, I immediately recognized them as cast members of the resurrected makeover show, Queer Eye. I'd been trying to interest Todd in the show in the hopes he might cultivate a more acceptable wardrobe, or at least one with less animal detritus. The results were less than hopeful, as you might've seen in the tabloids.

"That is the worst thing I've ever seen. And why does he have all those Berenstein Bears books?

"Wait, did you say Beren*stein*?" Hillary demanded.

"Yeah, look."

Hillary looked at the screen and shook her head.

"It's happening faster."

"Oh, sweetheart," one of them said to Hillary when he saw me. "I wish you'd said something, I would've brought the rest of my gear."

"Alright, calm down." I said. "What's the deal here, anyway? Since when do you guys do women's makeovers?"

"We don't."

"Hill," I said. Then I realized what they were getting at. "Fine, let's get this over with. We have a universe to save."

"We don't have much time boys." Hillary told them. "Do what you can in, let's say, fifteen minutes."

"You can't be serious. Fifteen minutes? I'd rather ride a unicycle with a bayonet for a seat post."

"Jesus Christ," I said, "you guys realize that I'm standing right here?"

"Okay," Hillary said. "Twenty minutes. But not a moment longer. Mister Palin here has a date in Switzerland in three hours."

"A date?" I asked. "You mean that scientist? Correct me if I'm wrong, but doesn't he think he's meeting Taylor Swift?"

"I still can't find her, so we're going to have to come at a different angle."

Twenty minutes later I looked at myself in the mirror, and didn't recognize the person looking back at me.

"You know what," Hillary said, appraising me thoughtfully. "I wouldn't have guessed it, but you don't look half bad as a man."

I had to agree with her. I mean, I probably won't keep the look in the long run, but I would've rubbed one out if I had the time and privacy.

"Nice work, boys." She said, checking the time. "Alright, we have to get to the airport. You guys be good."

"Should we watch the video again?" One of them was saying on our way out.

"You're sick!" Another gasped. "Honestly, there's something wrong with you."

The Lonely Scientist

His dancing video having made a strong impression on me, I recognized Frank Dunbar, the CERN scientist, immediately. I found him in the upscale Geneva wine bar we'd agreed on—well, that he and "Taylor Swift" had agreed on. He was sitting alone with a mostly empty bottle in front of him. Quickly checking my look in the glass door, I suffered a brief moment of panic, thinking I was about to be accosted by some rando. Except I was that rando.

He'd better have some wine left for me, I thought, pushing through the door into the bar. I approached his table and sat down.

"Sorry," he slurred. "I'm waiting for someone."

"If Taylor Swift gets here I'll be sure to give her my seat." I said.

He looked at me with a puzzled expression, which then gave way to an understandable look of disappointment.

"She's not coming, is she?"

"I mean, she might?" I shrugged. "Weirder things have happened. Weirder things *are* happening, actually."

"I guess it's pretty farfetched to really think Taylor Swift was coming to Switzerland to meet me. So, shame on me, I guess. Who are you, anyway?"

"If you'd asked me that yesterday I would've had a clear answer for you. But today?"

"I don't understand."

"Don't worry about it. I have my own things going on, which are none of your concern. What is, or at least should be, your concern is of much graver importance than my sexual identity or your being stood up for a date."

I didn't get the impression he was taking me seriously, so I showed him the video. He tried to pretend it wasn't him at first, but that didn't hold much water.

"Have you shown this to anyone else?"

"Aside from Hillary Rodham Clinton?"

"Why would….nevermind. What do you want from me?"

I told him all the pertinent information about the schism between universes, and how someone, likely from CERN, had figured out how to cross between.

"I knew about the schism," he said. "But I didn't know about anyone crossing over. I swear."

"Does the name Kelly Whitney mean anything to you?"

"She oversees the lab where I work. And she's been missing for several days. Is she okay?"

"I don't know." I told him honestly. "But it's vital that you get me into her lab. I need to see what she was working on."

He shook his head.

"She cleared her stuff out. All of it. There's nothing to find there, and you wouldn't understand it even if there was. No offense."

"That's why I have you."

"I wouldn't understand it either. Doctor Whitney writes everything in a kind of shorthand code. No one but her understands."

"Do you know where she lives?"

"Er, yes, I went to her apartment once. She told me that if I ever came back for any reason short of the apocalypse that she would use my balls as castanets. And I believe her."

"Frank," I said. "This is the apocalypse. Take me to her apartment."

"Did you hear what I said? Castanets! She's fucking crazy!"

"Frank, take me to Kelly's apartment or I'll cut out your balls *and* your eyes, and put your balls where your eyes are supposed to go."

"Jesus Christ, fine. I'll take you. But if she catches us

she's going to do things to your balls too."

"I don't have any balls."

"What the hell is going on?" He whimpered. "Ten minutes ago I thought I was going to meet Taylor Swift, and now I'll be lucky to keep my balls for the rest of the day."

"If it's any consolation, you wouldn't have fared much better with Taylor." I said, emptying the last of his wine into a glass and draining it in a gulp.

"That was a two hundred dollar bottle of wine."

"Thank you."

Doctor Kelly Whitney had a pretty swank place in Saint-Gervais, one of Geneva's finer neighborhoods, which might sound like a redundant thing to say. The door was locked, and as we expected there was no one to answer the door. Frank was visibly sweating as I picked the lock, and I had to physically shove him through the door. Once he was satisfied that she wasn't hiding somewhere with a pair of kitchen shears, he showed me her home office.

"If there's anything here, this is where it would be." He said. "But like I told you, she writes everything in code."

"Don't worry about that." I told him. "I'm fluent in a dozen different ciphers. Just look for dates. Anything from within the last month especially."

"Here's something." He said, pulling a notebook out from under the desk. "The last entry was dated a week ago. But like I said, beyond the dates it's all written in code. It's meaningless to anyone but Doctor Whitney."

I have to admit that I struggled with a slight flagging of confidence. What if he was right? If I couldn't decipher her notes, this trip would have been a waste of time, and would potentially mean the end of the world as I knew and tolerated it.

"Just give me the notebook." I sighed.

He handed me the notebook. I looked inside. Stared at the pages full of words and schematic sketches.

"I told you." He said, with a bit more satisfaction than seemed necessary.

"Code?" I growled. "That's not code, it's called cursive you fucking moron. Are you kidding me? Are you sure you're a scientist? Have you seriously never seen cursive?"

He started to cry. He looked so sad with his shoulders heaving inside his ill-fitting blazer that I couldn't help but feel sorry for him.

"Listen, baby, I'm sorry about the name calling." I cooed, rubbing his shoulders. "That wasn't cool. And to the extent that I'm capable of liking people, I don't hate you.

But seriously, man. Code? No wonder Taylor Swift doesn't want you."

"Are you saying that if I knew cursive, she'd want me?" He sniffled, dabbing his eyes with a handkerchief of questionable hygiene.

"No, I'm not saying that. No one's saying that. No one's ever going to say that."

I took the notebook and found the most comfortable looking chair. She only had one chair so it didn't take long. Her notes didn't read like those of a person in the grips of a psychedelic drug binge, and I had to remind myself that the version of her described in the emails was from the other side. Which also meant there was a possibility that it was the other version of her who'd discovered how to pass between, and if that was the case it was unlikely I'd learn anything of immediate value.

The logistics were giving me a headache and I went to the kitchen looking for a snack. I hadn't eaten anything since the enchilada incident in Hillary's cabin. I managed to scrape together some more or less edible cheese and salami, which complemented the stale crackers wonderfully.

Revitalized, I returned my attention to the notebook. To Dunbar's credit the notes were difficult to read, but from what I could tell it seemed that the portal was actually inside the apartment. Specifically, in the bathroom.

"Tell me something," I said to Frank, who was fastidiously tidying up the kitchen. "Does Doctor Whitney have some kind of preternatural fondness for bathrooms?"

"I'd say so." He nodded. "She insists on having her own private facilities at the lab, and even so she still sometimes goes home to, uh, well take care of business. Why do you ask?"

Normally I prefer to give only as much information as absolutely necessary, but these were unique circumstances.

"I think the portal might be in the bathroom."

"At CERN?"

"No, here."

"Seriously? Let me see that." He said, reaching for the notebook.

"I thought you couldn't read cursive."

"Oh, right. Well, theoretically she would need a tremendous amount of power. If there's an interdimensional portal in her bathroom it should be fairly obvious."

"What if she could tap into the city's main power grid? Would that be enough?"

"Maybe, why?"

I showed him a diagram drawn in the notebook, detailing her efforts to do just that.

"I guess we should take a look?"

With all the buttons and knobs and esoteric blinking lights that I would never understand, the scientist's bathroom had more in common with an experimental power station than my powder pink fortress of solitude at home.

Home. I missed it. The bathroom anyway.

She hadn't made any effort to hide what she was doing, which may have had something to do with the severity of her warning to Frank to stay out. Not that anyone would want him in their regular bathroom, either.

"What do you make of all this?" I asked.

He shook his head.

"I've never seen anything like it." He said. "Well, outside of the lab anyway. I take it your bathroom doesn't look like this?"

"Nevermind that. Can you figure out how it works?"

"Well, I believe you're supposed to sit here. You know, for as long as it takes…"

"I mean how the portal works, goddamnit."

"Right, right. Well, as far as I can tell, you'd have to get inside this chamber where the shower is supposed to be.

Which, the fact that she doesn't have a shower explains a few things, but that's beside the point."

"Get in." I said. "There's room for both of us."

"Get in? Hell, I'm not getting in there. We're just as likely to get fucking vaporized than to travel between parallel dimensions. Frankly, I'm still not a hundred percent that any of this is real."

I showed him the email transcripts between the alternate version of himself and the agent pretending to be Taylor Swift.

"Are you sure this is authentic?"

I nodded.

"So, if I decide to believe you, that means I've been tricked by people pretending to be Taylor Swift in two separate dimensions?" The sad look on his face told me he believed.

"I'm afraid so."

He took a deep breath and dabbed at his eyes a little.

"Fine," he said. "I'll get in. I don't really have much to lose, do I?"

"You said it, not me."

In a pleasant juxtaposition from the complexity of the outer workings, the interior of the portal was simple in the extreme. Just a single button. With the door closed behind us, I reached for the button. Frank grabbed my arm.

"Are you sure you want to do this?"

"I don't have a choice. Pushing the button might kill us, but not pushing the button would have consequences that can't even be measured within a known framework. Besides, if you help me save the world, I think that's the kind of thing that might impress adorable popstars."

Frank considered this.

"Push the button."

The Other Side

Nothing happened. I'm not sure what I was expecting, but it was definitely something. It hadn't even really occurred to me that nothing would happen. The weight of unfulfilled anticipation settled on my shoulders.

"Well, shit." I said, pushing open the door of the portal. If nothing else, it was nice to no longer be trapped in a tiny space with a strange man with liberal ideas on the subject of personal hygiene.

"Who knows," Dunbar said cheerfully. "Maybe a schism in the time/space continuum won't be such a bad thing?"

"I appreciate your optimism," I acknowledged. "But I don't share it. Now, if you don't mind, I need to take advantage of the more orthodox use of the room."

Dunbar blinked expressionlessly.

"Jesus, man, do I really have to spell it out for you?"

"Right. Sorry. I'll just be, uh, in the other room."

"Naturally."

As I sat there contemplating my next move, I realized that the walls were a different color than before. If we didn't solve the problem soon, it would be too late.

"Hey," Dunbar said as I closed the door behind me.

"Does something seem different in here than before?"

"The dimensions are merging. It's happening faster and faster."

"Huh…"

"What is it?"

"Well the cheese and crackers are all gone, for one thing."

"I took care of those the old fashioned way." I told him. "Anything else? You know the room better than me."

"Well there's a note here, written to Doctor Whitney, supposedly by me. But I don't remember writing it. And I certainly don't remember flying to the states to meet anyone. Which is what the note claims."

"Let me see that."

But as I was reaching for the note I saw something more compelling. A pool of blood gathering on the floor under the kitchen sink.

"Let me ask you something. Do you remember there being a bunch of blood on the floor? Doesn't seem like something I would've missed."

"No, I don't." Dunbar said, reaching for the cabinet door under the sink. He pulled open the cabinet and immediately let it snap shut. He suddenly looked so pale that I expected him to ask for my manager.

"What is it?"

His mouth open and shut like a fish struggling to breath, but he didn't say anything. I opened the cabinet and saw the body stuffed in there. It was Dunbar.

"So it looks like maybe the portal worked afterall?"

"She killed me." Dunbar said, a faraway look in his eyes. "She killed me and she stuffed me under the kitchen sink."

"Yeah. Pretty impressive."

Dunbar looked at me.

"I mean, nothing personal. But you have to admit, it is pretty impressive."

"I don't have to admit anything!"

"Keep your voice down." I told him. "I think I heard something."

"What did you hear?"

"Well I can't tell if you keep talking!"

"Who's raising their voice now?" He chided me. I made a mental note to punish him later. If there was a later.

A creaking outside the door got louder, and closer. I couldn't help but relish the thought of Dr. Whitney coming home and discovering Dunbar very much alive and not stuffed under the kitchen sink. But that wouldn't solve anything. I took a position behind the door and waited for the sound of a key being inserted in the lock. But that's not what happened.

"Police! Ouvrez la porte!" Someone hammered on the door.

"I don't think that's Doctor Whitney." Dunbar whispered.

"No shit!"

"What do we do?"

Getting caught by the Swiss police was not an option. Especially not with a dead body under the sink, whose exact double was alive and well. Alive, anyway. I grabbed as many of Whitney's notes as I could and hustled Dunbar back to the portal.

"I can't just leave myself down there," Dunbar said, struggling against my grip. "I'll just stay here and try to explain things."

"That's admirable of you, but I can't let you do it. We're going to need you on the other side if we have any hope of building a new portal."

"A new one?"

"Well we can't use this one anymore, can we?"

I had to manhandle the deceptively heavy scientist, and shove him into the portal. A project made more difficult by the stack of papers occupying one of my arms. Good thing I was arm-wrestling champion of Wasilla for three years in a row. Pageant winner and arm-wrestling champ. Talk about a double threat.

The door sealed shut with us inside, I pushed the button again. And again, nothing seemed to happen.

"What if they're still out there?"

"Hiding in here won't do us any good either way." I said, pushing open the door.

The walls were back to the slate gray they'd been before we got in.

"Thank God." Dunbar said, falling to his knees a bit melodramatically.

"Stand up, man." I told him. "I don't have time for your theatrics. I thought scientists were supposed to be calm, cerebral."

"Your little conceptual boxes can't hold me."

"Just cabinets and interdimensional portals, huh?"

"Where do we go now?"

"Well we can't stay here." I said, grabbing my phone and routing a call through an Order of Athena server. It was risky, considering our recent breach, but I didn't have time for other options.

"Operator." A voice said.

I recited my code-phrase and the line clicked.

"I have the package and need immediate extraction."

I was given coordinates to an unofficial airstrip outside the city.

"We're going to need a car." I said. "Where are you parked?"

"I don't have a car," Dunbar said sheepishly.

I saw a set of keys hanging next to the front door.

"What about Doctor Whitney?"

Dunbar nodded.

"If it's here it should be in the underground lot."

The strange whine of European police sirens emerged in the distance.

"We have to hurry." I threw all the notes I'd collected from both dimensions into a shopping bag and we took the stairs down to the basement. "Which one is it?" I asked, scanning rows of late model luxury vehicles.

"That one." He said, pointing out a rusty old Peugeot.

"Are you fucking with me?" I demanded, pleaded. "Please be fucking with me."

"Sorry?" He shrugged. "It wasn't my idea."

I could hear the sirens in the distance above us as I

maneuvered the brutally unresponsive vehicle up the spiraling levels of the parking garage and finally emerged into the open. The garage's exit was an alley on the rear of the building and the police hadn't yet formed a perimeter. Dunbar, dizzy from the drive, opened his door and vomited red wine onto the street.

"Jesus, man." I sighed. "Are you all done? Now tell me how to get out of here."

The Hostage Crisis

The cabin was seeming smaller by the second, and the man had had about all he could take from his hostage. She was now putting the final touches on her third mean song about him, and the blood that pounded in his ears from all the pullups and pushups didn't begin to drown out the annoyingly melodious sound of her voice. But he couldn't gag her because her tiny nostrils were insufficient for drawing breath, and a dead hostage wouldn't help him at all.

Not to mention that the president had proved significantly less vulnerable to humiliation than he'd imagined. It was becoming clear that he was going to have to re-strategize. But it was hard to focus when he couldn't stop humming the songs his hostage was singing about him.

"Could you at least stop making the songs so catchy?" He asked, in what he hoped was a conciliatory but still authoritative tone of voice.

"You do know who I am, right?"

"I guess that's a no, then." He sighed. "I'm going for a walk."

He'd barely left the cabin when a thought occurred to him. In all likelihood this so-called Order of Athena wanted the opposite of what he wanted, but there were certain elements of their disparate plans that dovetailed. Namely: they both wanted to get rid of Goldilocks. If he could convince them that he was also trying to sever the connection between dimensions, he might be able to get access to the underground lab. The question was how to contact them. His only hope was return to Hillary's cabin.

Exfiltration

As the plane lifted off the ground I looked through the tiny window and saw the police cars swarming the landing strip, their flashing lights shimmering through the fog. Dunbar's weak stomach had nearly cost us our freedom, and the rest of the world along with it. The cars got smaller and smaller and then I couldn't see them anymore. Couldn't see anything but clouds and emptiness, and Dunbar doing a little dance in his seat with his headphones on.

"What're you listening to?"

"Huh?" He asked, pulling off his headphones.

"I said, what are you listening to?"

"Uh, Taylor Swift."

"Right."

I sat there for a while, listening to the whine of the plane's massive engine, the blood in my ears.

"Hey," I said, moving seats and nudging the bizarre but not altogether horrible scientist. "You got an extra headphone?"

He grinned and pulled an earbud out, handed it to me. I put it in my ear and leaned back. Taylor asked me *'are we out of the woods?'*

Not yet, sister.

Back to the Woods

When we landed, the pilot handed me a note. All it said was 'back to the woods.'

"How long ago did you get this?" I asked him.

"I dunno, an hour ago?"

"An hour? And you're just now giving it to me?"

"What would you have done differently if I'd given it to you before?"

"Alright, I see your point. But still."

"Take it easy, man."

"Who are you calling *man*?" I demanded, then remembered my disguise. "Nevermind. Just have a car brought around."

"You need a driver?"

"No, I'll be driving. Where are we, anyway?"

"Upstate New York."

I checked my watch. I didn't like being out of the loop, but sometimes that's just how it goes.

The car was brought around and I told Dunbar to get in.

"Any chance you can put some tunes on?"

"Sure," he said. "Looks like the stereo has Bluetooth. What should I play? Taylor?"

I nodded. "You know it."

The drive wasn't long enough to get through the album, and I thought about taking a short detour to at least finish Bad Blood, but there were more important things going on than pop music, no matter how catchy.

When I pulled up to the cabin it felt like a lot more than a couple days had passed since I'd last been there. It gave me a weird, vertiginous feeling.

"You okay?" Dunbar asked me. I nodded and got out of the car, but I wasn't sure if I'd been lying. There were two other vehicles in the driveway. I recognized the Tesla Hillary had been driving, but I didn't know anything about the other one.

The door to the cabin opened and I reached for the weapon I no longer had. Hillary walked out like she was stepping off a plane. She was wearing a fresh pantsuit, possibly the finest one so far. Following behind her was some guy I'd never seen before.

"Looking for this?" Hillary asked me, handing me my favorite piece.

"Thank you," I said, tucking it in the back of my waistband. I'd never been able to do that before, with the tight skirts Sarah Palin is expected to wear. It felt pretty cool. I felt cool.

"So?" She asked. "Is this him?"

I nodded. "Don't you recognize him from the video?"

"I did," she admitted. "I was just trying to be tactful."

Dunbar looked at his shoes.

"Don't be embarrassed." She told him, rubbing his shoulders. "We all dance weird when we think we're alone. Look, before we go inside, I have to know. Did you find the portal?"

"We did." I told her. "Unfortunately, going back there isn't going to be easy. We've got half the Swiss police looking for us."

"What happened?"

"Long story." I said. "But essentially Doctor Dunbar here and his unknown male accomplice are wanted for murder, possibly in both realities."

"Sarah…" Hillary sighed.

"We didn't do it!" I assured her. "But when they find out that the body belongs to Dunbar, I'm guessing they'll narrow the search to the male accomplice. Either way, going back to the portal isn't an option."

"Can we make another one?"

"Not without access to the collider." Dunbar said. "And I'm not really allowed back there."

"So we can't use the portal," Hillary said. "And we can't make another one without access to the collider. And we can't access the collider."

"There was a rumor they were building another one,"

Dunbar said. "Somewhere in the states. But it never panned out."

"That's not completely accurate." Hillary's guy spoke up for the first time.

"This is Roger, by the way." Hillary said, looking at Dunbar. "He's the guy that catfished…well, he's a valuable asset."

"The computer lab where I work was originally built to accommodate a super collider modeled on the one at CERN."

"What happened?"

"Well, for security reasons the console that controls the collider was engineered to fit in a small, handheld device. Almost like a videogame. The console disappeared a little over a year ago."

"Let me guess: they either had to admit losing a device that cost tax payers millions of dollars, or just pretend it had never existed in the first place?"

"More like billions," Roger said, jamming his hands in the pockets of his coveralls. "But yes."

"If your collider is anything like ours," Dunbar said, "it would take up about as much space as two soccer pitches put side by side. What's being done with all that space?"

"I don't know what a soccer pitch is," the agent shrugged. "But the space is mostly used for storage. Old desk chairs, heavily redacted documents nobody wants to acknowledge."

I was reminded of something I'd seen in a photograph of the first family.

"Does anybody have a phone?" I asked.

Roger handed me one. I looked up the photo I'd seen. Melania squinting into the sun, the president looking vapid and flabby, almost like he's not quite sure where he is. But most importantly their youngest son, playing with a handheld videogame that appeared to have a phone plugged into it.

"Does the console look anything like this?" I asked. Roger looked at the photo, paled, nodded.

"Are you telling me a child stole a billion dollar piece of top secret equipment, and nobody even noticed?"

"Well, I mean, we noticed." He said defensively. "Eventually."

"Jesus Christ." Hillary snapped. "So the hacker we've been moving against is just some kid playing a videogame…"

"Hold on a second," I said. "Why's everyone so down? This is good news. We just have to get the thing back from the brat, and build a new portal using Doctor Whitney's specifications."

"I've been looking over the schematics, and I don't think that making a new portal is going to help us." Dunbar said. "In fact, it could make things a lot worse."

"Okay, so what do we do, then?"

"As far as I can tell, we need to reproduce the collision that caused the rift in the first place. But I don't know if I can do it by myself." Dunbar admitted. "But you work at the lab, right?" He asked Roger. "You can help me."

"Sorry." The agent said. "I can probably come up with a dildo and a sandwich, but I don't know the first thing about engineering."

"What else would you be doing down there?"

"Cyber espionage." He said. "Which sounds a lot cooler than it is. Basically, I email tragic sad-sacks, pretending to be women way out of their league. Getting them to divulge information they never would have if they weren't so tragic and sad."

"Huh." Dunbar grunted, looking at his shoes.

"Holy shit," Roger said, a flicker of recognition in his eyes. "It's you, isn't it?"

"I don't know what you're talking about." Dunbar insisted. "I would never leak privileged information, even if you really were Taylor Swift. Shit."

"Nothing personal, man." The agent said, patting Dunbar on the back.

"Hey, don't worry about me. I don't even..." he started to cry a little.

"Would it make you feel better if I introduced you to the

actual Taylor Swift?"

"Don't fuck with me, man. You might be able to fool me once. Maybe twice. Three or four times at absolute tops. But I'm not falling for it again."

"Let's go inside." Hillary told everyone. "There's something else I need to show you. Or rather, someone else."

The Plan

Nobody was more surprised than Dunbar to actually find Taylor Swift sitting on the couch. Personally, I was more shocked to discover the man whose interdimensional twin Hillary had dispatched just a few days earlier. He and Taylor were laughing hysterically, which I thought extremely odd, until I realized they were reading Goldilocks's diary.

"What can I say?" The man said. "I clearly misjudged the guy."

"What the hell is going on here?" I demanded. There were too many new variables all at once. I felt dizzy. And hungry. I noticed Dunbar hovering near the door, staring at the lithe popstar. I gave him a little elbow. "Snap out of it, man." I hissed. "You're coming off like a weirdo."

Taylor must've heard me because she looked up from the journal and saw Dunbar.

"Holy shit!" She said. "Is it really you?"

From the way Dunbar's face lit up he clearly thought there'd been some kind of misunderstanding, and that it really had been with her that he'd shared such intimate correspondence.

"Doctor Frank Dunbar." He said in what I can only assume was his professional voice.

"You're the guy from the dancing video!" She shrieked, clapping her hands with unmitigated pleasure. "Hillary was just showing me!"

"Is there anyone who hasn't seen the goddamn video?" Dunbar demanded, his professional tone abandoned for one of shame and grief.

"We've only watched it a few times, my dude. Don't get so worked up. If you'd just owned it we'd consider you a hero."

"Really?"

"Yeah. Of course, it's a little late for that now."

"Is someone going to explain to me what he's doing here?" I snapped, jerking a thumb at the dude who in less than a week had abducted every woman in the room.

"It turns out our goals aren't so different." Hillary said, with what might've been a just barely perceptible wink. A wink I chose to interpret as *we're just messing with this dude and you have carte blanche to do with him what you will.*

"I've been corresponding with the president for close to a year." The man said. "I convinced him that I was developing a new and extremely effective hair growth treatment, and he's been funding me."

"What was your plan in case he found out you were lying?"

"I had what I thought was dynamite blackmail material.

Turns out I overestimated his capacity for shame."

"So why are you here?" I asked. "What exactly are you bringing to the table?"

"I realized it was wrong of me to use an interdimensional crisis for personal gain. I just want to help."

"That doesn't answer my question. And while I'm glad you've found Jesus or whatever, I still don't see why I shouldn't kill you right now for what you did to McCain."

"I didn't kill him, I promise. Though, I might've tricked you into killing Valerie P."

"Why?"

"Well, she was going to kill you, if that concerns you at all."

"Because you tricked her into it?"

"Everybody slow down," Hillary commanded. "We have more immediate concerns. Like, taking a fake president out of the White House and sending him back where he belongs."

"Hell?"

"Close," Hillary said. "Professional wrestling."

"There's something I still don't understand." I said. "At a certain point, for whatever reason, what should've been a singular timeline split into two, and we here in Berenstain-Goldilocks world got the raw end of the deal."

"Right."

"The schism. Are we calling it schism? What're we calling it?"

"Schism, paradox, whatever, what're you getting at?"

"So are we trying to join them back together? Or like, subsume the other one? Because, unless we have a time machine, I don't understand how we can undo the trauma already inflicted. And if we rejoin the timelines, won't that effectively be like, killing everyone in the world? Or in one of the worlds, anyway?"

"Right!" Taylor jumped in. "Wouldn't it be better to just sort of separate people into the worlds where they're a better fit? Like, I have a very hard time believing that I was meant to live in a world where Trump is president and Kid Rock exists. But some people must belong here?"

"I see where you're going with this," Hillary nodded. "But aside from the ethical considerations, there's a problem of logistics. I can barely make it through a shopping line without someone having a violent episode. Can you imagine trying corral the entire population of the world? It would be like a Black Friday sale to the millionth power. Our minds can't even comprehend it. We'd be looking at mass annihilation."

"That's actually a good idea." Taylor said. "Black Friday. Everyone who goes to a mall the day after Thanksgiving gets to live in 20!8, or however you pronounce that, and the rest of us get the Berenstein world we deserve."

"Hold up just a second there, Sister." I said. "Just because somebody likes a good deal and maybe even enjoys the brutality of a massive sales event doesn't make them a bad person."

"Doesn't it?"

Obviously, I'd already considered the possibility that I was meant for 20!8. That I'd lived in my cover for so long that I'd come to embody the ruse. Or, even worse, that I'd always been that person. I didn't like this thread. I was more or less a good-ish person, beneath the persona, and I also didn't think I belonged in a world where the orange bastard was president. I belonged in a world where one of my Sisters was president and the Orange Bastard was a retired professional wrestler who lived alone in the desert and ate beans for dinner (granted, I made some of that stuff up).

"Ideally," Dunbar interjected, studying Dr. Whitney's notes. "When we fire up the second collider, given the complementary meridians, it'll simply be like none of this ever happened. It won't be time travel or murder, things will just be like they should've been. But that's assuming the collider caused it in the first place, and that any of this makes any sense at all. Which…"

"The Hadron Collider was activated in what, two-thousand-eight? Will we have any memories of the years between. Of this?"

"I don't know."

"And there's another thing that's been bothering me." I said. "Whatever caused the schism, it had to have been within the last ten years, or so. Right?"

"And?"

"Well, why do some people have totally different lives, going back decades?"

"Look, Sarah," Hillary snapped. "We really just need positivity right now, so if you'd rather obsess over details than save the world, you can just go wait in the car."

"Can I listen to the radio?"

"AM only."

"Fine, I'll be quiet."

"I'm not trying to be negative here," the kidnapper said. "But can we even get access to the underground lab?"

"Don't worry about that." Hillary squinted at him. "And how do you know about the lab, anyway?"

"I heard you talking about it outside. And the diary."

"Which, by the way," Taylor frowned, holding the book at arm's length. "There's something gross all over it."

"My dog threw up on it."

"Your dog has discerning taste."

"Agreed". Hillary. said. "Now, this is what's going to happen. Sarah, you drive the boys to DC. Take my car, it's faster. Taylor and I are going to rally the troops to create a diversion, giving you the opportunity to grab the console. You think you can overpower the kid and take his favorite toy?"

"I practically live for that kind of thing."

"Good. Take this radio. We're going old-school. When the time is right, you do your thing. I'll tell you where to bring the console."

"How will I know when the time is right?"

"You'll know." She said. "Believe me. Keep in mind, we don't have time for subtlety or worrying about consequences."

"Perfect." I said. "Also," I added, lowering my voice so that only she could hear me. "What should I do about Goldilocks? You want me to…you know…?"

"I like where your head's at," Hillary told me. "But no. There are things in this life that are worse than death, and those are the things I want for him."

"Gotcha." I said, gathering myself and stashing the radio in my jacket pocket. The quantity and size of pockets available in menswear was hard to wrap my mind around. I don't know how—or if—I'll ever go back.

"However," Hillary added, grabbing my arm and pulling me close. She smelled like a secret flower garden in a children's book and I had to pinch the skin on my forearm to concentrate on what she was saying. "If you have an opportunity to slap him around a little…just, enjoy yourself is all I'm saying. Just not too much. I'll need him cognizant for what I have planned. As cognizant as he's capable of being, anyway. As for the abduction enthusiast, you know what to do."

Pistol Whip

Dunbar and the agent were in the backseat, with the kidnapper up front where I could keep an eye on him. Roger was still apologizing to the scientist, and the kidnapper was singing some song under his breath.

He was a mean man/with a stupid plan/can't do anything right/just does what he can.

He stopped when he realized I was looking at him.

"So," the man said, scratching his knee. "Are we really going to just shut the whole thing down? Aren't you curious about the paradox? What it might mean, and what we could do with it?"

"It doesn't interest me in the slightest." I said. "I've already had more than enough goddamn interdimensionality. Speaking of which, how the hell did you cross over?" I asked the man. "Or like, the other you, or whatever."

"I honestly don't know," he said. "He found me. I was just trying to do some pullups and eat some chicken one day, and all of a sudden there he is. I thought I was going crazy. Even God is crazy, I guess."

"Nevermind that." I said.

There was no time for subtlety, or for considering consequences. It was pretty liberating for someone like me, who has no subtlety and never thinks about consequences anyway. Speaking of which, I pulled the car to the side of the road in a remote area north of Virginia.

"I need to know something. What would you have done if I went back to your hot tub with you? Were you trying to kill me?"

"Of course not," he said. "I needed you to take me to Hillary. I might've even gone down on you."

"Get out." I told the kidnapper, showing him the business end of my pistol.

"But why?" He stammered. "I thought we were working together?"

"Why? Because fuck you, dude. That's why. Now get out. Hillary told me not to get any blood in her car, but I think she'll forgive me."

"Fine." He said, putting his hands up. He reached for the door handle but tried to fake me out and grab for the gun. I smacked him hard on the bridge of his nose, which started to bleed profusely.

"My face!" He screamed, shielding himself with his hands. "Not my beautiful face!"

His attention diverted, he didn't notice when I implanted him with a tracker.

"Goddamnit!" I gasped when I saw his blood getting on

the car seat. "Look what you've done."

"I'm sorry." He whimpered, his eyes watering. "I'm… not very good at any of this anyway. I'll just go back to being a successful venture capitalist I guess."

He got out of the car and as I pulled away I saw him standing there with slumped shoulders and I almost felt a little sorry for him. Then I remembered all the women he'd abducted—myself most importantly—and I nearly went back to hit him again.

"That seemed kind of harsh." Roger said from the back seat.

"You want to join him?" I asked. "Now somebody move up front. I'm not your goddamn chauffeur." The agent tried to climb through the seats. "Not you," I told him. "Dunbar, get up here."

As we approached the city I thought about what I would say to Melania. It wasn't the first time I'd had to confront another parent about something stupid their asshole kid was doing. But usually it was, like, throwing pinecones at our cat. Or throwing pinecones at our dog. Or throwing pinecones at the baby. Point is, almost always pinecone related. So how do you approach the First Lady and tactfully suggest that her son had hacked the time/space continuum? Awkward! I had no frame of reference, and as far as I knew, neither of the

Landers had ever discussed it. I considered writing a letter but realized I didn't have that kind of time to play with. Besides, I'd already written them dozens of letters and they'd never responded.

The Bear Parade

Apparently they remembered me at the Victoria's Secret. Specifically, they remembered me locking myself in the dressing room for hours, though they didn't seem to recall how I'd been the first goddamn woman Governor of Alaska. Either way, they tried to physically block me as I made my move back to the dressing room. Normally I might've had to waste precious minutes fighting off three assailants coming at me with pointy shoes, but the trousers I was still wearing made for unusually easy locomotion and I was able to launch myself off a display table and crash through the door of the dressing room and through the secret passageway before they even knew what was going on.

I ran down the long hall and reached the final door. Taking the radio out of my pocket I sent a test signal. But I didn't get a response. Either something had happened to HR or I was too deep in the tunnel to get a signal. If there's one thing I know it's that Hillary Rodham can handle herself in combat, so it must've been the tunnel. Whatever she had planned, it wasn't going to be possible to let me know. I was going to have to make my move, go in blind.

Alright, Sarah, this is it.

The Key was still in the door from last time, and as I

pushed the lever I saw light coming through the painting behind it. I didn't hear anything, but I saw a shadow fall across the canvas. Taking a couple steps back I sprinted forward and launched myself through the painting, landing in a roll and slamming into the back of a sofa. When I stood up, my weapon at the ready, I saw a small boy sitting on the sofa opposite me. He was staring at me expressionlessly, his inscrutable eyes glowing with some kind of chained up intensity. There was an intelligence in his face that clearly derived from genes not belonging to the president. He was squeezing the console in his pink little hands, knuckles already going white in anticipation.

"I'm gonna have to take that from you." I told him. He said nothing, but slowly, almost imperceptibly, shook his head.

To hell with it.

I made my move, and we wrestled over the device for a while. I thought it'd be easier to beat up a little kid. It always had been in the past, anyway. But this kid had some kind of superhuman strength, as well as a little Harry Potter wand he kept jabbing me with. Which, as I've said before, Sarah P. does not enjoy getting jabbed, even if only for a few minutes at a time, once or twice a month.

Finally I knocked the kid down and messed up his little pompadour. Unfortunately the console got pretty banged up in the melee, but I didn't have time to think about that because the door to the oval office opened and Melania came in. She looked at her son, trying furiously to fix his hair, and then at me, engaged in a similar enterprise. Unfortunately for me, it didn't take a genius to figure out that something untoward was happening.

"Sarah? Is this you?"

"Is *that* you." Her son corrected her.

"Go finding your father." She told him, and he ran out of the room.

"I realize this must seem a little strange," I said, jamming the console in my jacket pocket. "But I assure you it's necessary, to reverse the schism."

"I'm sorry, Sarah," she said. "But I can't let you do it."

She had my scarf that I'd left in the car after shopping, and the other hand was holding a stapler. She was kind of pointing the stapler at me in an aggressive manner.

"Why the hell not?" I demanded. "And what's with the stapler? Are you threatening me?"

She looked at the stapler in her hand.

"I was already holding this." She said. "But I'll use it if I have to. You see, my son doesn't exist in the other timeline, and he's the only thing in the world I care about. Aside from outrageous couture fashion, of course."

"I'm sorry." I told her. "But I have my orders, and I'm

pretty sure The Order would notice if I didn't do my job."

"I've never done any job, and nobody seems to care."

"I think we're comparing apples and oranges here. Speaking of oranges, I have a presidency to erase, so either take your shot or get out of my way."

"Please," she said sadly. "In other timeline am nothing but cheap prostitute."

"And here?"

"Here? Am very expensive prostitute, obviously."

"I see what you mean," I admitted. "But we're all making sacrifices. In the other timeline my husband is a good man who wears clean clothes. You think I'm happy about losing that?"

"Is hardly fair comparison."

"Well, I guess you have a point, but that doesn't change anything." I said, making a move for the tunnel.

Melania blocked me and stapled my scarf to my shoulder blades. Which, since I keep losing it, she was doing me a favor. Besides, it was sort of cape-like, and flapped pretty majestically as I ran back and forth in front of the mirror.

Turns out I wasted valuable time looking at the mirror because the door opened and the president came in, preceded by a strange smell. Goldilocks himself, his signature funk flooding the room. A combination of smoked pork, gastrointestinal effluent, and tanning oil. I reached for my pistol, but then remembered what Melania had said about his fontanelle. I wrested the stapler from Melania's hand and lunged at the president. His head looked like a massive block of fuzzy cheddar, and I swung the stapler at what I hoped was the vulnerable part. The stapler connected, but rather than kill him immediately as I'd hoped, there was just an innocuous tapping sound, like chopping onions on a plastic cutting board.

"You fool!" He laughed, clapping his tiny little hands in wretched glee. "Did you really think I'd leave my Achilles heel vulnerable?"

"You're pretty smug for an amorphous blob of flesh." I said, letting go of the stapler, the teeth of which were embedded in the helmet he was apparently always wearing under his wig. "And frankly, I'm surprised you know who Achilles is."

"I pulled a tendon in the bathtub this spring, but that's beside the point." He said. "What exactly is the point, again?"

"It's the bears of Berenstein!" Melania shrieked. "It's paradox! We have to stop her or we lose everything. We lose our son!"

"What the hell did you say about bears?" He demanded, turning a slightly redder shade of orange. Like, safety orange. "I'll put a stop to that right now. Where are my brass knuckles?"

While he patted himself down looking for his miniature custom made brass knuckles, I edged my way towards the tunnel.

"Stop her!" Melania screamed.

"Fuck it," he grunted, giving up the search. "I'll stop her with or without my knuckles. Nobody's bringing bears around here on my watch."

"Also because you'll lose your son," Melania added. "Right?"

"Which one?"

"Barron!"

"Oh, yeah. I'm gonna need him to look after me. I can't count on the other three. Derrick and Jason, and whatever her name is. The hot one. The main thing is I won't allow any bears whatsoever. Even paradoxical ones."

He moved to block my exit. I reached for my gun. I've reached for it too many times lately without getting to use it. I flipped off the safety just as the door burst open and two secret service agents tried to fit through at the same time and got stuck in the threshold.

"Mister President!" They both shouted, angling for position in the doorway.

"What I'd tell you about sneaking up on me!" He barked. "Can't you see I'm busy?"

The agents looked at him, and at the stapler stuck to his

head. They looked at me in my cape, and at Barron lying on the floor, still trying to fix his hair. For what I can only assume was the first time in Donald Trump's life, his hair wasn't the most fucked up in the room.

"Mister President," they repeated, their brains apparently refusing to accept the reality of the situation. "There's a disturbance on the lawn."

"What kind of disturbance?"

"If you'll just look out the window, Sir…"

"No! Describe it to me!"

"Sir, there are what appear to be several hundred bears on the lawn."

"What?!" He screamed, running to the window. "You have machine guns, right? Everyone has machine guns?"

"Affirmative, Sir. However, we're pretty sure they're not actually bears. We have reason to believe they are actually people in bear costumes."

"You lie!" The president gasped, clawing at his ridiculously long tie. "Shoot them!"

"Whether or not they're actually bears, the optics of killing them all could be devastating. Even for this administration."

"They're coming right at us!" Goldilocks croaked, diving under his desk with far greater agility than I would've thought possible. It was like an overweight Guinea pig diving into an empty roll of toilet paper.

I took the opportunity to make a break for the tunnel. I didn't look back to see if anyone was chasing me. The tunnel was dark and I couldn't see anything, until I burst through the door into the Victoria's Secret and crashed into a couple who were having sex in the dressing room. I'd rather not say anything too specific about that moment, or its aftermath. The point is, old Sarah P. came through in a big way, with barely any body fluids to speak of.

1989

The commotion in the Victoria's Secret gave me the cover to slip out mostly unnoticed. I guess two naked people in flagrante were more compelling than a one-time presidential hopeful dressed up as a man with a sartorial flair for capes. I circled around the block and doubled back to make sure I wasn't being followed, and was about to use the radio to contact HR when a large bear came around the corner and headed straight at me. When I reached for my gun the bear took its head off. It was Hillary. Looking around, I noticed there were even more bears than I'd realized. They were everywhere. Swinging on lampposts, jumping on cars. It was madness.

"What the hell?" I asked. "Where in the world did you come up with hundreds of bear costumes all of a sudden? You must've had this planned..."

"For months." She said, using one of her paws to push the hair out of her eyes before putting the head back on. I will never underestimate her again. Though I feel like I've said that before, so probably I will at some point. "Come with me." She told me. "You have the console?"

"Uh, yeah." I said, showing her the device, which as I mentioned was a little worse for wear. Luckily she couldn't see well enough through the bear head to notice.

We went down a short alley, at the other end of which Dunbar and Roger were waiting in the car. The agent had managed to acquire security passes for the three of us.

"It was actually really easy." He said. "Like, almost disappointingly easy. There's practically no one around. Everyone either already quit, or just don't give a shit."

"Alright, Sarah." Hillary told me. "It's all up to you, now. Go with them to the lab and make sure Dunbar follows the schematics. Our world is counting on you, whether or not they know it."

"I'm pretty sure that having a lifesize bear tell me that the world is depending on me is something I had a nightmare about once." I told her. I couldn't see her face. Just the placid expression being worn by the bear costume. But I'd like to think that she gave me some kind of knowing smile. A smile that was meant to fill me with optimism and a sense of purpose.

We encountered virtually no resistance as we entered the federal building that was a decoy for the lab deep underneath. I knew my gun wouldn't set off any metal detectors, but I wasn't sure about the console. The detector blipped momentarily but nobody seemed to notice.

Entering the elevator, Roger used his badge to access the lower levels, and we slowly descended. I noticed Dunbar was holding a bag, presumably with Dr. Whitney's notebooks. The elevator took so long that for the first time in a long time I had an opportunity to start doubting the plan. What if we started the collider and nothing happened? What if things actually got worse? I didn't have time to visualize the more explicit scenario that 'worse' might entail, because the elevator stopped and the door opened.

We were in a mostly uninhabited computer lab, lit only by the glow of dozens of unattended screens. The agent motioned for us to follow him along a corridor of empty chairs.

"The collider is housed even farther below ground, and it can only be accessed by a separate elevator." Roger said in a low voice. Then, in an even lower voice, "I'm not even sure it works…"

"I'm sorry?" I said. "What was that last thing?"

"Shhh," he told me, holding an index finger to his lips. "We're going to have to sneak past the front desk area."

We came around a corner and I saw two men, one sitting at a computer, one standing over his shoulder.

"So you're telling me the future of our world as we know it depends on Taylor Swift? Who we can't even find?" One of them said, pacing back and forth.

"Well…"

"How did we get here?"

"Nineteen-Eighty-Nine is a really solid album…"

"That's not what I'm talking about, and I think you know it. If we don't solve the problem, we lose our reality. But if we admit that there's a problem at all, we lose our jobs. I don't know about you, but I have bills to pay, and frankly I don't care if my house and clothes change color now and then, or if I can't find anything in the kitchen. Besides, if we solve the problem we might end up with a boss who actually demands results. The answer seems pretty obvious to me."

"Well, can I keep catfishing this guy at least?"

"Do whatever makes you happy, man. I'm gonna go get blackout drunk, try to forget about all of this. I think there's a game on."

"What game?"

"Who fucking cares."

The man slumped off, leaving only the one sitting at the computer. He was pretty focused on what he was doing and we were able to make our way past him and into the second elevator. Roger swiped his security badge again, but nothing happened.

"Huh." He said.

"Huh?! What do you mean, 'huh'?"

"Well, I mean…" he swiped his card again. The doors still didn't close. He swiped it a third time and an alarm went off, and the guy at the computer turned around and looked at us.

"Rog? Is that you?" The man asked. Roger kept swiping his badge, with no discernible improvement to our situation. "Roger, what the hell are you doing?" He squinted at me in the dim light. "And is that…is that…Sarah Palin? Dressed up as a man? What the hell is going on here?"

"Did you say Sarah Palin?" The other man asked, reemerging with a bottle of scotch. "Holy shit, it's you! Sarah Palin," he repeated my name, apparently getting pleasure from merely pronouncing the words. "I'm your biggest fan!"

"Well you're a fucking idiot then." I told him. The last thing I saw as the doors finally closed was his face, obviously wounded on an emotional level.

"Out of curiosity," Dunbar said. "How many fake romantic relationships are you guys carrying on down here?"

"So many, dude." Roger shook his head. "So many…"

"That should make me feel better, I guess.

When the doors opened we were in an indefinably large space that smelled of cement and dust, the damp cold hanging heavy in the air, clinging to me like an unwanted boyfriend.

"We're not going to have much time," Roger said, leading us along a pathway around what must've been the collider itself. "Despite appearances there are still security guards around here. They have guns, and they're eager to use them."

"I know the feeling." I said, listening to the reverberating echo of our footsteps clattering in the darkness.

Finally we reached a lit area with a large bank of computer stuff I couldn't understand.

"You have the console?" Dunbar asked me. I handed it to him, crossing my fingers it would still work.

Dunbar fitted the console into a port on the computer and everything lit up. Rows of lights ticked on in two wide arcs until finally the entire sub-basement was brightly illuminated. It was much larger than I would've expected, though since I didn't know anything, my expectations weren't worth much.

At the end of the corridor from where we'd come there was a commotion. Roger had jammed the elevator doors with something, but it didn't seem like it was going to hold.

While I was distracted, Dunbar body-checked me. Another thing I hadn't expected. He got my gun away from me.

"Dunbar?" I said. "What the hell are you doing?"

"This was the whole point!" He shouted, pointing the gun at Roger and me.

"*What* was the whole point?"

"This!" He said, opening the bag he'd been holding and taking out a dildo and what looked like a Reuben sandwich.

"Have you lost your mind, man?" Roger asked. "I assumed you were joking about that."

"Seriously," I added. "Even *I* know you can't just collide random objects."

"I'm the one with the gun," Dunbar shrieked. "I'll collide whatever the fuck I want!"

"You can't really believe that you caused a schism in the time space continuum by colliding a dildo and a goddamn sandwich." I sighed, watching the world as I knew it drift away before my eyes.

"I guess we'll find out, won't we?" He said, loading the objects into two compartments on either end of the computer bank. I figured I could probably overpower him if I wanted, but I kind of just didn't care anymore. It was all a roll of the dice at this point, anyway, and I was tired. As much as I enjoy kicking asses, sometimes I'd rather take a bong rip and sit back with a chilled rosé, watch some Bachelorette.

"Is that even the right kind of sandwich?" I asked, patting myself down for an emergency cigarette that wasn't there.

He gave no indication of having heard me. The system began to power up, a deep thrumming sound issuing from the depths of the collider. Security guards at the end of the corridor had managed to pry open the elevator doors and were running towards us with what I assumed were fully automatic MP5s. I could hear their boots hitting the cement floor, getting closer. Either way, our journey was almost over.

I spent the few seconds I had remaining thinking about my family. Nevermind the fact that they'd been part of my elaborate cover identity, they were real people. They were my real life. Their flaws were the blooming flowers in my life's little garden. It was a shitty garden, maybe, but it was mine. If I failed them, I failed myself, and everything else I'd done was worthless.

For the first time in as long as I could remember, I wanted to live. I seriously, savagely, wanted to live. I wanted to go home.

Suddenly there was blinding flash of light, and a sort of vacuum anti-sound, as if all sounds were being sucked into a black hole. I recalled a similar sensation from previous blackouts. This time, I figured I was dead.

I'm walking through a forest at night. I can't see anything, but for some reason I'm not worried. I somehow know I'll end up where I'm supposed to be.

The soil's ancient rime cuts through me, permeating me. The way a forest smells. Something about fresh cut pine, so fresh it's nauseating.

I sense the air is cold, but I don't feel cold. I don't feel anything except relief. A weightlessness. My thoughts drift.

My childhood house, memories black and white, waiting for my dad to get home. My dad the school teacher. I was just a kid back then, and life was all spread out before me, and everything seemed possible. Where am I now?

I'm becoming like mist, floating up. Nothing can hurt me, nothing can touch me.

No more sounds. No more faces. No more staring at the mirror, trying to figure it all out.

It's all figured out, now. It's all perfect. Everything is perfect.

I see lights, colors. The night sky glows and glasses my eyes to blankness and everything is perfect.

I'm coming home.

Homeward Bound

The light that filled my eyes was so bright, so penetrating, that it was almost like darkness. The fragrance that filled my nostrils was like a field of wildflowers, and I knew I must be dead because nothing on Earth could smell so much like heaven.

I heard a sound being repeated, and I realized it was a name. It was my name. I felt my body being moved, but I didn't try to struggle against it. I was at peace with whatever was happening.

I heard my name again and opened my eyes. It was Hillary. She smiled at me, and I tried to smile back.

"Please don't make that face again." She said. "Whatever it was."

"I remember you," I said. "I didn't forget…"

I laughed, and became aware of myself, my limbs, my body. These were the real things. The things that mattered. That things that bothered me before: the ignominious fates that await true heroism. The gruesome portraiture. The pornographic tributes. None of that mattered.

"Are we okay?" I asked.

Hillary helped me to my feet. We were at an outdoor airstrip, I didn't know where.

"You tell me." She said. "What even happened down there?"

"I don't really know." I said honestly. "I think Dunbar was tripping on acid. I think he slipped me some too. He didn't actually care about healing the schism or whatever. On the plus side, I think he healed it anyway."

"Let's just call it another one of those weird little things." Hillary said. "But just imagine what he could accomplish if he actually set his mind to it."

"What's left of his mind, at least. Where'd he go, anyway?"

"He got away. Snagged one of the bear suits and took off on foot."

"Somewhere there's a man-sized bear running around with a head full of acid. I'm guessing we'll hear about it in the news."

The winter sun was bright but cold, and the wind that blew across the field surrounding the tarmac stung my eyes. I felt alive.

"What's going to happen, now?"

"I've done things." She said. "To protect the Order, the Sisters. Everything I've done has been for that, and I would do it all over again. But that doesn't mean I won't pay a price for it. I would spare you that price. Besides, you deserve a break from being Sarah Palin."

"Be that as it may," I sighed. "I have to go home. I have a feeling that my family needs me."

She smiled and nodded.

"Go home." She said. "Be with your family."

"Thank you." I said, and walked unsteadily towards the plane. Then my feet stopped, and I looked back. I wanted to see my friend one more time, in case it would never be like this again.

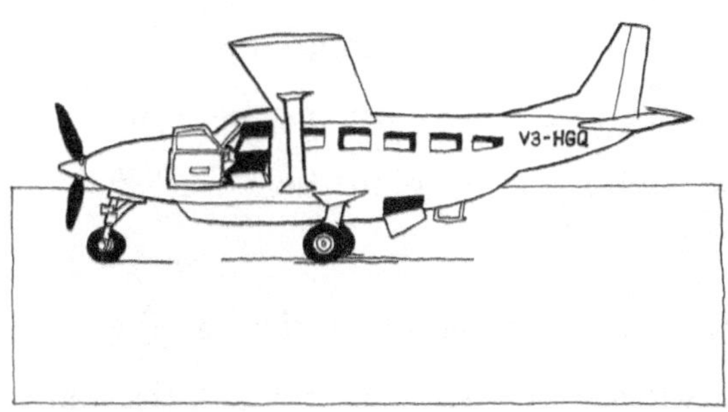

Home Alone

When I got into the car that was waiting for me at the small airfield about forty-five miles northwest of Wasilla, there was a note on the steering wheel. It was from HR, thanking me for my help and promising a tropical getaway at the earliest possible convenience. Which, for a person as busy as Hillary could mean anytime, or never.

Flying over the Gulf of Alaska and all the little islands, I'd had an uneasy feeling. Maybe I didn't believe that we'd really succeeded. Or maybe I just didn't want to believe it. If it was really over, then what purpose did I have? I hadn't spoken to my family in well over a month, and they were apparently fine. Or at least as fine as us Palins ever are. They were used to me disappearing for long periods of time, and they'd learned to get along without me. If my family didn't need me, and the Sisters didn't need me, what value did I have?

It was winter now, and I cut through the deep drifts of snow that flanked the sides of the road, the boughs of the trees so heavy that it nearly blinded you to look at them, the green needles struggling to poke through. As much as I love cranking up my snowmobile and feeling the crisp air in my face, I wished it was spring. Spring has always been my favorite time of year. The newness, the rebirth, the outdoor keggers.

The feeling that I'd had on the plane came back to me, and I wondered if I'd get to experience another changing of the seasons. Whether it would really be me, or some version of me. I wondered if my family would be better off with this other version. It made me feel something like jealousy, and I pushed on the gas, my headlights flashing on the road as it carved through the forest and eventually opened up on our town of Wasilla. I'd been born in Idaho, but it was Wasilla where I'd been formed, where my memories had been created, and where I'd become the person I am.

Driving through the town now, down the old streets, all the familiar sights of my childhood flashing past me, it felt—not like I was seeing them for the last time—but like they were already gone. Something in me knew that it was time to move on. This place was no longer for me.

I pulled over at the Foodmart to get a bottle of wine. Walking through the doors I felt a little better. The familiar smells: cheap perfume, rotisserie chicken, and shellfish. I'd hoped to run into Kelly, and apologize to her. If that was still possible. But I was told she hadn't been to work in a few days, and that nobody knew where she was. She always said she was going to go and see the world, and she must've finally done it. I felt happy for her.

When I finally pulled up to our house it felt like I hadn't been there in years. Even Levi's truck, parked diagonally and taking up two spaces, didn't bother me. I saw that the Christmas lights had been put up, and even though it was still early afternoon they twinkled brightly in the dim winter light. I saw a Christmas tree through the window and my heart sped up in anticipation of seeing my family.

I was happy to see my family, so something had definitely changed.

I opened the door and called out, "I'm home!" But nobody answered. I put down my bags and looked around. The house was empty except for the dog, whose name was Monkey. He seemed scared, and wouldn't come out from under the kitchen table. Where the hell was everyone? I checked all the rooms again. Bristol's door was closed, and despite her warnings, I pushed it open and turned on the lights. I could smell a faint whiff of the Febreze she uses to cover up the sex smell. It doesn't help.

I went upstairs and sat on the bed, looking at myself in the mirror. I was still dressed as a man, and the already frenzied state of my hair had been exacerbated from sleeping on the plane. I looked like Edward Scissorhands.

I listened to the silence in the empty house and felt so lonely I could've fired up my snowmobile and taken it to the edge of the flat world I supposedly believe in, sometimes.

Then I saw the note taped to the mirror.

If you want to see your family again, come to the place where you ruined my life.

-Kelly W

Theoretically there could've been a number of places that would qualify, but I knew that she was talking about the basement rec-room in the house where she'd grown up. Where I'd seduced her father—and brother, and boyfriend…

Alright, Kelly. Let's play.

While rifling the drawer for extra ammo I found an old jewelry bag with a little blow leftover from Todd's birthday party. Should I? Probably I shouldn't, but I figured I would just do a little bit while I considered it. After that the decision was easy. I dumped the last of it out and cut it in two lines. But the dog ran and jumped on me. He was the first dude I'd been happy about seeing in a long time.

I was somewhat less enthusiastic about the fact that I'd spilled cocaine on his head. Gumming coke off a dog's head. I'm not proud of myself, but fucking hell, a woman's got needs, especially when she's trying to save her family and the universe. I scratched the dog's neck as I licked the top of his head, him leaning into my fingers, his neck lolling. Then, just when the moment threatened to become cloyingly sweet, he bit me. He always knows when to bite me.

I fed Monkey and filled his water bowl, took a few swigs

of whiskey, and left the house. While making the short drive to Kelly's parents' house I saw Garth/Goth walking on the side of the road. I drove past him and stopped, then backed up. Watching his image grow large in the rearview, I'd planned to get out and grab him by the lapels and tell him his name was Garth. Garth!

But when I saw his face, I couldn't do it. Maybe it's a sin to rob others of the delusions that keep them going. Sometimes it's all they have. Hell, I'd just licked cocaine off a dog's head, who was I to judge? The world is a brutal place, on its best day. If people need to tell themselves little lies to keep getting out of bed in the morning, who am I to deprive them?

"Hey, Goth." I called out through the open passenger side window. He looked over, squinted at me through the wan December light. "You need a ride anywhere?"

"Hey, Sarah." He said, taking a drag from a cigarette. "Nah, I'm okay. How're you doing, anyway? I heard Kelly was looking for you."

"I'm on my way to see her now." I said. "You think I could bum one of those?"

He approached the window and put his head in. Goth Noir. He was a good guy, and he deserved better than the small life he'd been allowed. Maybe we all did. He handed me a cigarette and we stayed there like that for a minute, not saying anything.

"Guess I'd better get going." He said, finally.

"Yeah," I said. "Me too."

"Merry Christmas, Sarah. Your hair looks awesome."

"Same to you," I told him, lighting the cigarette. "And listen. Just…just take care of yourself, man. It's good to see you."

"It's good to see you too." He said, and started walking again. I watched him disappear in the snow.

The Long Road to the Beginning

Kelly's parents' house hadn't been lived in for years, and was dark when I pulled up outside. But I saw a faint light glowing from the tiny basement window where we used to spy on her brother. I knew from experience that the window was big enough to squeeze through, but fuck that. I wasn't squeezing through anymore windows. I was going to kick the front door down.

The front door turned out to be sturdier than I remembered, and kicking it down was impossible. Fortunately, it was unlocked. I checked the action on my pistol and went inside. No point in sneaking around, as anybody inside would've already heard me kicking the door. The house was quiet and dark, but I knew my way through its small rooms and hallways as well as I knew anything. When I got to the basement I saw my family, all tied to chairs. Even Levi was there. I felt something swell in my heart, and I didn't care about the danger. I ran to them.

There was something hot about seeing my husband tied to a chair and I sat on his lap, straddling him and taking the gag out of his mouth to kiss him.

"Whoa, buddy!" He said, winking at me. "I like girls!

One in particular."

"You better be talking about me." I told him, kissing his face and neck, which barely had any deer blood on it. But enough that I knew it was really him.

"Eww, Mom." Bristol, who was tied up next to Todd, gagged. "What the hell?"

"Jesus, can't we ever get any privacy?"

I was so happy that I nearly forgot why I was there, and I didn't notice the person approach me from behind.

"I'm so glad you could make it." Kelly said.

I stood up and turned around, looking at my old friend. Then I had to wonder if I'd drunk more whiskey than I'd realized—or possibly there were some lingering effects from Dunbar's LSD—because another Kelly walked up and stood next to the first one.

"So," I said. "It was you, afterall."

"Of course it was me." The first Kelly said. "When I crossed over, the first thing I did was track down my alternate self, which turned out to be disappointingly easy. I couldn't wait to find out what kind of amazing things she'd accomplished, and when I discovered what you'd done to her, and the life she'd been reduced to, I made it my primary mission to return the favor."

"Kelly," I said to the second Kelly, the one I'd grown

up with. "I was in a bad place back then, and I treated people badly. You more than anyone, I guess. You didn't deserve that, but I don't know how many times I can apologize for what I did."

"Well, once would've been a fine start!" She sputtered.

"I'm sorry."

"Now? You must be joking. We're lightyears beyond that now."

"So what is it that you want?"

"First, I'll take that gun from you."

Alternate Kelly had a shotgun, which she kept trained on me as my old friend relieved me of my other friend.

"What else?"

"I want a child."

"I said I was sorry, and I am. But you can't have my kids. I'm not even sure why you'd want them. No offense, guys."

"I don't want *your* child," Kelly said. "I want a child of my own. And I want it with your husband."

"Him?" I asked, looking at Todd in confusion and disbelief. "Are you sure about that?" It seemed too easy. But then I realized that even if it was that easy, I wasn't going for it. "You know what, no. No matter what I've done, you can't have my husband, even for the few minutes it would take."

"Huh, okay." Kelly said. "What about him?" She pointed at Levi.

"That's up to my daughter." I said. "Bristol?"

"What?" Bristol asked, intently picking fingernail polish off her cuticles. "Yeah, whatever."

"Do I get a say in this?" Levi asked.

"No." I shook my head. But then he gave me one of those sad puppy faces for which I've repeatedly proven myself weak. "Okay, fine. What do you say?"

"I'm okay with it." Levi said cheerfully, then tried to lean in to kiss Kelly. But he wasn't sure which one to kiss, so he tried to kiss both of them. They both leaned back.

"Whoa," both Kelly's said. "No touching necessary."

"Oh," Levi sighed, clearly disappointed.

"What's this really about Kelly?" I asked, looking back and forth between them, as I was no longer sure which was which. "You can't expect me to believe this is about harvesting second rate genetics. No offense, you two."

"Huh?" Both Levi and Todd grunted.

"You're right about that." Kelly said. "Or at least half-right. Believe it or not we've been on the same team the whole time. I was the first to discover the split timeline, and the first to create a portal so that I could move between them. The first thing I did was track down the alternate version of myself, thinking who else but myself could provide the best support? Never in my life would I have expected to find her still living here, working at the Foodmart. To say that I was disappointed would be the world's greatest understatement. No offense, Kelly."

Kelly frowned but said nothing.

"You really did a number on her, Sarah. However, because of our diverting life experiences, your old friend Kelly here managed to avoid having the same car accident I did. An accident that made it impossible for me to reproduce. And since I'm now stuck here, we're going to raise our child together. Speaking of which, congratulations on your success with the schism. I have to say, I underestimated you."

"You can thank Dunbar, if you can find him. I suspect he's clinically insane, but he pulled through at the end. Or at least the version of him you didn't kill. What was that about, anyway?"

"He tried to shove his hand down my pants. Came over with some sob story about Taylor Swift, went all fifty shades on me."

"Good for you." I told her. "So where do we go from here?"

"Well first I just need a little…" Kelly produced a syringe and deftly took some blood from Levi, who barely seemed to notice. "And the other thing is…well… we think it's about time for you to leave Alaska."

"What a coincidence." I said. "I've been thinking the same thing."

"One more thing," Kelly said. My Kelly. "Despite what I said earlier, I would really appreciate an apology."

"I'm sorry, Kelly. I really am. I know it's unforgivable, and I don't expect forgiveness. Looking back now, it's hard for me to imagine what I did. Seducing your dad, and your brother, and your boyfriend…"

"You slept with my boyfriend, too?!" Kelly gasped. "Which one?"

"Nevermind that." The other Kelly said, rubbing her shoulders. "It's ancient history, right? Only the future matters now. And that future is right here. Well, not right here, exactly. Wasilla is a shithole in every possible reality, and I don't plan on ever coming back."

"Well whatever you two do, I wish you the best." I said. And I meant it, mostly. "So, we can leave?"

"Please do." The Kellys said.

I started untying my family. I still didn't know quite what was going on, but I'm used to that.

"Just one last thing," Kelly said as we were leaving. "What kind of name is Trig, anyway? I've always been curious about that."

"I told Bristol she could name the baby. Asked her to think of a smart name, and Trig is what she came up with. It's not quite what I had in mind, but a promise is a promise."

"Fair enough."

"By the way," I stopped. "Merry Christmas, you two."

"Just go!"

"Yep."

The End of Something

I woke up to the sound of the surf gently lapping against the seawall below my window. I was alone, but my family was safe, and the mental security afforded by that fact was a much better thing than having to actually hang out with them. In the ephemeral moments between sleep and the other thing, I lay back with my eyes closed and listened to the ocean, inhaled the pleasing tang of brine and the remnants of tequila in the glass next to the bed.

What we had accomplished was unequivocally the greatest feat in recorded history, and almost nobody would ever know about it. The women do everything and nobody cares.

Fucking typical.

I'd heard that the satisfaction of doing good was contained in the act itself, and that only an immature person acted in pursuit of external reward. I wasn't buying it. I wanted people to know, and I didn't care if that made me immature. I didn't want to be some kind of wise rat living in the sewer, teaching kindness and ninjutsu to mutant turtles.

Oh, well. I certainly wasn't going to go against HR and my sisters, especially not after being let into the inner circle. I would just have to learn to be spiritually graceful and self-contained, as incredibly boring as that sounded.

Rolling onto my back I found the remote and turned on the TV. The remote wasn't even chained to the nightstand, like it was in all the places Todd wanted to stay. Talk about luxury.

When I saw the image that appeared on the screen my heart nearly stopped. A hideous man with orange hair and orange skin was yelling into the camera, the greasy folds of his neck skin flapping as he shook with rage, spittle and what looked like bits of rotisserie chicken flecking off of him. But it wasn't possible. This couldn't be. My hand trembling, I turned up the volume to hear him.

"In an incredible upset, The Undertaker has just come out of retirement and defeated the undefeatable Back-Alley Boys, single handedly! Believe me, Folks, nobody saw this coming. Least of all the Back-alley Boys…"

I muted the TV. He was even harder to look at in silence, if you can believe that.

Sitting in the front row just behind him were Melania and their son. Her Russian handlers had lied to her. Apparently they were meant to be. A match made in hell.

"Good fucking God," I sighed in relief, laying back and unclenching my jaw. I looked over at the inch or so of tequila in my glass and emptied it in the general direction of my mouth.

I was apparently already wearing my bathing suit, so I grabbed a towel and a few beers and headed down to the beach. Oprah and Hillary were already there, and I dropped myself into an empty barca-lounger next to them.

"Sarah," Hillary said, lowering her oversized Jackie-O sunglasses and fixing me with one of her looks. "Would you care to address rumors that you've not only written a book of some kind, exposing secrets both national and Athenal, but that you're planning to actually publish it?"

"What?" I said. "No, of course not. I would never."

"Good." She replied, lowering her shades and leaning back into her barca. A few seagulls flew by overhead, stalking a child who was being careless with his banh-mi.

"Let's just say, theoretically, I *had* written such a book." I mumbled. "And in this highly fictional scenario, let's also say that I'd already spent the advance. What would, uh, happen, exactly? Theoretically?"

"Theoretically?" Hillary repeated. "I'd say theoretically you might find yourself stacking cans of pork-n-beans in hell."

"Please," I begged her. "I can't go back to Wasilla."

"Oh, leave her alone." Oprah said, swatting at a mosquito. "Anyone with half a brain automatically believes the opposite of whatever Sarah Palin says. Her publishing an exposé about the Sisterhood will only make us more secretive, if anything."

"Did you have something to do with this?" Hillary asked.

"I might've helped find her a publisher." Oprah admitted. "You should really read the thing. Funny stuff. Nobody will believe a word of it."

"You've actually read it?" Hillary demanded. "And you didn't say anything to me? I know how you love secrets, but when we get home we're going to have a serious conversation…"

"This is lovely." Oprah interrupted, rubbing prodigious amounts of coco butter into her unbelievably youthful looking thighs. A group of college age people walked by, all of them bronzed and beautiful, as if they were extras in a movie about high-stakes beach volleyball. One of them looked over at us, lifting up her sunglasses to see us better, but I saw no flicker of recognition in her eyes.

"Aren't you afraid of being spotted?" I asked Oprah.

"Are you kidding?" She asked. "I nearly got arrested for looking at a handbag a few years ago."

"Oh yeah, I remember that."

"So, Hill." I said, taking another shot at the nickname. "Are you okay with still not being president?"

"Yeah, I'm okay. It's for the best. Michelle is going to be great, and I could use a break. Afterall, no-bless no-bligé, am I right?"

"That's right."

Another group walked by, even lovelier than the previous one.

"Usually I hate vacations," Oprah said. "You go to these beautiful places, full of beautiful people, but you're only there because you're already in a relationship. Imagine. If someone on my staff pitched me an idea as asinine as that, I'd have them fired immediately."

"It's like going to a buffet on a diet." I said.

Oprah squinted, was silent for a moment.

"No," she shook her head. "I like it better the way I said it."

"You're probably right," I admitted. "'I'm no wordsmith. Just a secret agent with sixty-nine kills and forty-two cock-punchings under my belt. Besides, I kind of just saved the world."

"I don't deny any of that," Oprah sighed. "However…"

"You guys, I'm sorry to interrupt," Hillary interrupted. "But what color are these chairs?"

Oprah and I looked at each other.

"Red."

"Weren't they blue a minute ago?"

Coming Soon: 20!9

A forest compound deep in the Alaskan wilderness. A secret laboratory whose mysterious purpose includes creating an army of hillbilly clones. Levi, the perfect every-dude.

An Island paradise. Unchanging. An oasis from the time schism.

It was supposed to be a new year, goddamnit. A year of long hot baths and cold rosé, trashy television, a few good naps. But when I got the phone call that woke me from my aquatic slumber, my bathwater cold, my rosé tepid, I knew I wasn't going to get off that easy. Chances were I wouldn't get off at all, unless I could convince my house boy, Philip, to trim his fingernails once in a while.

"Who dis?"

"Hello, Sarah. It's me, Sarah. We need to talk."

"If you're really me, then you know those are my four least favorite words."

She knew, she just didn't care. I thought I'd found a way to live my best life in this shitty timeline, but things were worse than ever. And now I was getting threatening phonecalls from myself. I had a feeling 20!9 was going to be another fucked up year. Hopefully Hillary won't get mad at me for writing another book...

about the author

Anita Lobo was born in Houston, Texas. She enjoys reading, sleeping, playing tennis, and pretending to hate social media. She also loves Portland, Oregon, but she promises not to move there. Probably.